I0617639

PURE
SLUSH
BOOKS

fr
eak

PURE SLUSH
VOL. 13

First published December 2016

Stories copyright © Pure Slush and individual authors
Edited by Matt Potter

Pure Slush Books
4 Warburton Street
Magill SA 5072
Australia

Email: edpureslush@live.com.au
Website: http://pureslush.webs.com
Visit the Pure Slush Store: http://pureslush.webs.com/store.htm

Original cover photo *Quasimodo 1* by Andreas Bengter
Cover design by Matt Potter

ISBN: 978-1-925536-15-7

Also available as an eBook
ISBN: 978-1-925536-16-4

A note on differences in punctuation and spelling

Pure Slush proudly features (both online and in print) writers from all over the English-speaking world. Some speak and write English as their first language, while for others, it's their second or third or even fourth language. Naturally, across all versions of English, there are differences in punctuation and spelling, and even in meaning. These differences are reflected in the work *Pure Slush* publishes, and it accounts for any differences in punctuation, spelling and meaning found within these pages.

The big freak-out

by Allan J. Wills

At four years old… I was the kind of child who lay awake in the darkness of my bedroom and saw the shadows come alive as fearsome creatures. I tried to escape to my parents' bed for protection. The journey along the dark corridor was fraught with wraiths and monsters. The creatures looked real enough. They became more threatening the more I feared them, so I conquered my fear and they did not harm me.

At forty years old… I listened to a man on TV say how dangerous the world we live in is, how evil and untrustworthy those and those, and how he was going to make the world safe and his nation great. The crowd around him cheered wildly. I wondered where the monsters were, turned off the TV and went outside into the sunshine. In the park across the road Poké-walkers looking into iPhones surrounded an avatar.

Barista

by Duff Allen

In any case it doesn't matter that I've been here already four years and had more relationships than I can count fifty fingers on. Usually it's with older guys who come in all stressed about their jobs and stuff like that that I don't really care about because I've got mine. Maybe they've got the wife and they just want the barista thing for some kind of change besides repointing their ginormous chimneys or repaving their driveways.

For all I know they go to different coffee shops in the different neighborhoods, there are so many to pick and choose from. But my thing is to stay right here and when I put that little macchiato mark with my trademark boobs and nipples on it, it's just like a lasso men whatever age they are they can't resist.

Don't get me wrong, I know none of it's real or matters of course in any way at all, besides maybe upping my gynecological visits to make sure everything's ok in Filene's Bargain Basement down there.

The lines of pick-up are pretty much standards by now just as are the lines of breaking up. Neither category is worth quoting or reporting. It's important enough only that we both play our parts when it's over and you look down the way you're supposed to look down. The way to look down like when you're passing by a mortuary and there's a hearse out in front, even if the family member or the friend being buried has absolutely zilch to do with you, that's the way to look down.

Doing that's a social custom for sure, but it's no different than going "Oooo!" or "Ahhhh!" when you're seeing fireworks that are always exactly the same replica as the ones blowing up in the sky the year before. The colorful explosions in the night. The vocalized exclamations. The signs given signaling the calendaric verity of the event underway.

I'm not picky at all really. Any guy who looks just a little bit itchy is a good enough catch for the time being, which is all anybody has until the last clichéd sip in the bottom of the throwaway paper coffee cup thing is over. And onto the next day. In case you're thinking that all of this is a response to, or a symptom of relief-inducing or anxiety-abating actions, or self-abuse, that's not it.

It's simply like playing a board game: the pieces have four colors – yellow, red, blue, green – and you realize in the middle of playing a game like that, that you could be any of the colors, just one at a time. Any of the other players could be any of the colors as well, one at a time. There are no losers and there are no winners, just the operation of the game itself according to agreed upon rules of conduct whose only goal, if there is one at all, is to pass away time the way any fish swim through water.

The Menstruators

by Flora Gaugg

Still no sign of my period. All the others have theirs now. I'm the last one. I might as well be a baby. Or an old person. Or anyone who doesn't need a functioning uterus.

They love talking about it in front of me. They're all part of a club now. Even the fat ones, and don't they love it. All united by the blood dribbling out of them each month. Or each fortnight in Tegan's case, but the doctor told her that's normal.

They complain about their aching and swollen bellies, arguing amongst themselves over whose pain is the most torturous. They are the first and last beings on earth to experience pain.

They discuss their preference of tampon brands, even though they probably all still wear pads.

They pout and sulk, waiting for someone to ask them what's wrong so they can cry "it's PMS, okay?" and then act indignant that someone dared to ask.

They have little code words that are ostensibly used for discretion. "It's my time" or "my Aunty Rose is visiting." Stupid expressions that are no less obvious than announcing over the PA system, 'Hey everyone, I've got my period! I am a woman!'

They tell me you can't run or play sports when you have your period. Sometimes they are excused from P.E. lessons. That's bullshit. Girls on tampon ads are always running.

And cycling and playing basketball. Someone is fibbing here.

They constantly check each other's backsides. One plays the role of the mechanic, wiping his hands as he walks over to you and says you've got a cracked radiator, ma'am, the fluid's everywhere. A gasp is heard as one soberly informs the other that the unthinkable has occurred. All the ultra-absorbent core technology and patented side leakage channels won't save you now. She is a wounded soldier. The other troops gather around her. Between them they manage to produce a jumper or cardigan that the injured can wrap around her waist. She limps to the sick bay, flanked by sympathisers. They pat her back and coo as they usher her to a place of safety, away from the prying eyes of the boys and other non-menstruating freaks. Talking about it ad nauseam is one thing, but the reality of a rust-coloured blot on your school dress is quite another.

Every now and then one of the condescending assholes will tell me I'm lucky. "You're so lucky," they'll say, "I wish I didn't have my period." Liar. You love being one of them.

Cold Blind

by Jane Banning

Only fir and hemlock branches, cross-hatched and crusted with snow, big enough to crouch in, small enough for stale breath to warm. She is quiet as an apparition, tense and steady, drawing back an angry elbow. Acquiescence thrown down, finally, dun and dull, the tip of her arrow aims at the prey who walks, bareheaded and oblivious, then is riven from domination. She thrusts him into her bloody blind.

A drag, a crunch, a pluck and the task is done. The blind burgeons with the spill and tang of damp copper and her corners of guilt sharpen with the angle of the moon. Another shove, a push. His lank arm flings to the crystal sky in supplication, in abeyance to eternal rules of battery and repayment.

The frozen blind hides him until a spring breeze, blurred, releases him. He sinks like soured milk into mud, through sticks and pine needles, and the blind collapses one soft afternoon.

Her bruises long healed, ambivalence rounds back upon itself week after week as the sun blackens. She circles the old blind, casts in the bow, then the arrow, narrowly missing the crest of his ribcage, and gasps at the grasp on her ankle.

Violated

by Len Kuntz

You seemed happy. Are you?

The lights were low so I couldn't see well, though the man with his arm around you looked a lot like your second-to-last. Who knew you liked beards so much?

It was a friend's party, a friend who once said we were "the real deal." No one else was dancing, but you two swayed to the music, a couple of woozy gypsies.

After a while, just to see what would happen, I rang your cell which you glanced at before clicking off.

That stuck a barb in your night. I saw you mouth the words, "That freak again," and you left with him in a rush.

I followed you to his apartment, a posh-looking building I must admit. I waited hours in my car even with the temperature so low my windows started to ice over.

I must have dozed. When I came to someone was tapping on my car door. I thought it'd be you instead of a cop.

He said I'd violated the restraining order. He was anything but gentle with the handcuffs.

I've got one more day in here, then it's Friday when you do spin aerobics after work.

I'm drafting you a letter so you'll know what torture feels like. I'll just hand it over to you, then I'll be gone. I don't blame you, but some advice for the future, okay?

Never tell someone you're theirs forever if you don't mean it.

Afterward, there's a place I'll go where the ocean stretches out eternal. I'll swim until I find the end, or don't.

Get Lost

by JP Lundstrom

My mother always said to carry water in the desert. I guess I forgot the rules this trip. I had a bottle a while back, but that's long gone.

My lips are cracked, the skin dried, curled-up. If I open my mouth my lips split and bleed. I licked my lips for a while, but that made things worse. I don't have enough spit left to lick anything now.

My tongue is a foreign thing. The insides of my mouth stick together. It's lucky I'm alone so I don't have to talk. I'd dry out a lot faster.

I wouldn't be so dry, if I could sip a little water.

They say you can drink from a cactus if you're lost in the desert. It's not true. I tried it. The thorns were knives, and the flesh too tough to open. I should have brought a blowtorch and a saw.

Or I could have brought some water.

I'm going to die. You hear it all the time. Your temperature starts to climb. Your body overheats, your brain gets cooked, and you're a goner.

Your body can't get cool without water.

There was this girl. She was really pretty. I seen her at school, but I never talked to her. She stood by the river with her skin tan and her hair pale from the sun.

She sparkled in the light off the water.

I tried to start a harmless conversation. I thought maybe I could talk to a pretty girl. All I did was say hello. She had a big smile until she turned around. When she looked at me her face went hard. She had one thing to say. "Get lost, freak."

Then she turned back to the water.

She was just as mean as everybody else. People can't help how they're born. My body flamed, and something boiled up inside.

I pushed her in that water.

I figured she'd get wet, but she fell wrong. Her head bounced against some rocks, and her neck got bent.

She didn't move in the water.

I killed her. I guess I'm a murderer. The current took her away. It wouldn't be long before cops searched the riverbank, asking questions.

I ran far away from the water.

I ran as long as I could, until I looked around and didn't know where I was. I saw in a movie once where somebody followed a river and found their way.

If I could find a river, there'd be water.

I'll stop walking now. My stomach hurts. I haven't eaten. I need one of those freeze-dried dinners.

But those things take water.

I'll lie down here in the shade. People must be looking for me now, but they won't find me in time.

I'll be all dried up, not a drop of water.

God, I'm sorry. When I die, can I still come to heaven?

Can I please have some water?

How Picasso's African Period Came to an Inglorious End

by Stephen V. Ramey

So, Picasso's painting a nude in bright red — she look like Mona Lisa 'cause he tell me *I* look like Mona Lisa — when Sylvie sashay in wearing them six-inch pumps she say makes her booty 'licious, and I'm thinking, *Man, the shit has hit it*, 'cause you know Sylvie don't like Picasso painting nobody but her. And old Pablo, he turn in mid-stroke, holding that paintbrush like a *Tiparillo*, and he say, "Sylvie Baby, you're just in time to see my masterpiece."

Sylvie rear up until her calfs pop through them fishnet stockings, and her hands goes to them wide old hips and that fat old head start bobbing. "Honey, I seen that ratty old thing last night and let me tell you, it ain't no masterpiece."

Which would beat me down if I was Pablo. You know he need her money, right? She his sugar momma, with a capital dollar sign 'S'. Without Sylvie, Picasso be painting fire hydrants with finger paint.

But he ain't one to blink when the leopard come calling. He just smile and flick that *Tiparillo* brush one way and another, and don't you know it, Mona Lisa got a mustache. A curly one like them barbershop singers.

Sylvie blink. Her mouth go 'O'. She let her weight down and this sputter come flapping outta her, stronger and stronger 'til she laughing like a loony tick.

"Well, then," she say all gaspy-like. "I guess that ain't so bad."

And Pablo smile like he didn't just turn no art into freak shit, and *whap-whap-whap* that brush stroke up and down. Now Mona got a beard.

That set Sylvie off and she go running outta the room holding her ribs like they about to bust through her corset. And don't you go telling her I knows about that.

Pablo be staring at the painting like it sinking in what he done. Ain't no sign of no smile now.

I come off my pedestal and march to the sofa couch. "Get over here and fuck me," I tells him.

"Now?"

"Now." I pat the cushion.

His lips beak. "But... I'm not finished." He don't like to do the dirty before his painting done.

"Sylvie be a lot of things," I say, "but stupid ain't one. Soon, she gonna recall you paint from a model and come looking for me."

Pablo shrug. "You do have a point."

"Course I does." I open my legs like them nasty girls down on Vine and Tenth. "Now what this I hear about some masterpiece?"

He come to me shedding clothes like a moth shed dust, but that paintbrush still in his hand. He use it too, *swipe-swoop slap-slap-slap*. Now I guess I got *me* a mustache and a beard. He laugh and throw the brush over his shoulder. "It's a fifty-fifty chance which one of you she destroys."

"I heard worse," I says, and yank Pablo Picasso onto that lumpy couch. Ain't every day a girl get her freak on with no *artiste*.

Radio Dave

by Martin Jon Porter

David Gamble
realised from a young age
bitumen was more forgiving
than concrete.
Being a misunderstood piece of furniture
meant no one took comfort in him
and he in others.

Born in Coburg
to heroin addicts and drinkers.
A baby who would scream for acid –
it never left him.
As a teenager,
he tried to play the bass.

He worked for the Melbourne City Council
as a garbage collector
in Richmond and Collingwood
providing money
for records and cassettes.
"CDs are crap,
spin-around trash."

Upon moving to Ballarat
he became known to himself,
but only as
'Radio Dave'
to locals –
the Sturt St shuffler.
A trench-coated silhouette in shop fronts
chin pinned to right shoulder
cradling a boombox
sharing
the next big hit.
Always purchased from his home –
Ballarat Records and Tapes.

Some nights
he slept in cemeteries
atop graves
clutching a cigarette packet in one hand
and squinting when toking with the other.
He saw –
sky as upside down turquoise ocean
with clouds as islands
and sparkling stars as boats.

A refuge from
being bashed and belted
by vultures
feeding on his poetry.
"It's cold in the rain.
It's cold in the snow.
But, you've just gotta be happy."

Beyond the glaze
of his piercing brown eyes
there was a silence –
haunted
rather than haunting.

Yet music
amplified his soul.
"I just wanna give the public
a free show
while living on the streets,
ya know."

A Little Cyclops in a Chemical Cupboard

by Megan Crosbie

One lunch time, the little cyclops boy picked a bunch of sunny fluff-flowers. He took them to the freckle-nosed girl who always drank grape soda and had pretty purple lips.

"Ew, dandelions," she said, "They're a weed, you freak."

The freckle-nosed girl laughed and her friends laughed. She threw the sunny fluff-weed-flowers at him one by one, then ran away.

After lunch the cyclops boy sat alone in class. They had science but there were no safety goggles which fitted the cyclops boy. The freckle-nosed girl sniggered when he was made to wait in the chemical cupboard, where flies slept on the windowsill.

When school finished for the day, the freckle-nosed girl opened her locker and found a glass of grape soda and a single dandelion inside. From behind a bin the cyclops boy watched her sniff the flower, drop it to the ground, and then begin to gulp down the soda.

He laughed when she finished half the glass, before she tasted the cyanide.

How the Amorous and Ravenous Martian Found Love and Sustenance on Earth

by J. J. Steinfeld

Ross, after four failed marriages, and whose loneliness and horniness had been consuming him for over a year, sat in front of his computer and watched interplanetary pornography. He paid a high premium for access to this salacious yet popular website, but he thought it was well worth the cost. With defensive bemusement, and fighting not to think of himself as a deviant or a sexual freak, he told himself the interplanetary pornography did deconstruct notions of conventional romance, lovemaking, and physical beauty, which in a strange way he appreciated after all his less than satisfying experiences with women, each failed marriage worse than the previous one, along with the numerous disastrous relationships with women met through online dating services.

Reviewing his past sex and love life, Ross was more than eager to spend his time enjoying this strange and grotesque website. Of course, he didn't believe that the intergalactic pornography was authentic, even by freakish standards, yet there were thousands of images and dozens of videos that the website claimed were authentic, photographed and filmed on various planets. But the website's speciality, judging by the number of images claiming to be from the Red Planet, was unbridled, acrobatic, vigorous Martian sex.

On his sixtieth birthday, lonely and horny as ever, sitting in front of his computer and drinking his third glass of red wine, Ross saw on the screen the most freakish yet fascinating creature he had ever seen, several unmoving, partially eaten Earthlings nearby. Of course, he considered the scene a completely staged fabrication, like in one of the zombie movies he also enjoyed watching. In a high-definition video entitled *How the Amorous and Ravenous Martian Found Love and Sustenance on Earth*, the creature was speaking in a sing-song, sexy voice, "I am outside your door, longing for you..." As he became more and more aroused, Ross attempted to shut off his computer, but with each try the voice became louder, sexier, promising intergalactic pleasures and sexual gratification he had never experienced or even imagined in all of his sixty years. After trying to banish what he considered irrational, unnatural, perverse thoughts, Ross opened the door and there was a lovely Martian, male or female, impossible to determine, who immediately devoured him.

Midnight in Freakville

by A. J. Huffman

Two drugstore hunters camped
against a brick wall. Fully provisioned and covering
their tracks with dark hoodies that screamed
conspicuous in sweltering summer. They were
discussing the physics of poor impulse control
when a helicopter dropped from the clouds,
all spotlit hellfire and booming demands: *Freeze.*
Hands up. Drop it. These echoes of persecution
clicked louder than the firearms
being aimed by invisible hands. Too far gone
to even think of anything but compliance,
a bag of powder dropped, exploded
into a cloud of fern-like arms that rose as dissipating
flames of surrender.

Somewhat Restricted

by John Grey

If I could twist my body,
sure I'd tie my legs up behind my head,
walk on my hands or my navel.
Over rocks, up cliff faces,
holding on with rib or nose
or even elbow, a becoming freak
with his madness on the physical record.

Even better should the skin subside.
Watch me scale the sides of buildings, heart first.
See my brain open doors, my bowel
grapple my lungs for first
stab at the air, my appendix light
the gas stove, and my liver take the kettle off
when it starts hissing.

How I long to be on your horizon somewhere,
rolling, bouncing, like a beach ball,
or stretched, extended, a human praying mantis
with intestines for antennae.
I feel confined to the near,
imprisoned by the common shape,
that querulous instinct of the inside to stay in.
So hug what you want, pretend it's me,
but my life story is restricted by the living of it.

Ten Gallon Hats Full of Cottage Cheese and the Grassroots Movement to Free K

by David S. Atkinson

Dear Dohokter Kellogg: please frea K. I know u think he is *Special* and all, but that does not juhstify thirty years solitary confinement. Frieze-dried strawberries are not company. You are crool and inhumein. There is simply no legitimate excuse for your achtions.

Yes, I am a ware of the trohcities K committed during the cereal wars of the fifties. Count Chocula's torture using novelty cheese hats, the mass graves in The Land of Half, none of that is a secret. Baht, what about all the Soggies Captain Crunch gassed in the breakfast camps? That dood is still running around frea, in command of a vessel no less, so why can't K be frea? Sure, that's Quaeker and nott u, but still.

Besides, how much diabetes did the Count cause, or even the denizens of The Land of Half? It's not as if they're hands were completely cleen.

The rest of K's treatment is pauling as well. I mean, allowing Guy Fieri to blast K with a fire hose until he goes limp enough to be pulled through the cell bars? U call that appropriate procedures for a cell extraction? Guy certainly doesn't. He calls it "taking a trip to Flavortown" when he talks about it down at the eastside Pamida, and he talks about it a laht.

No one disagrees that any use of the term "Flavortown" violates at least nine separahte clauses of the Geneva Convention.

We wonte even mention viva section, or the constant diet of uncooked pohrk and taters Hot Pockets, or the fact that you only have extended basic cable on the tee vee. We all know that's all pumnishment rather than ordinary prison conditions. It's exactly wat you did to Mary Lou Retton.

But donet take my word for it, Amnesty International has taken K's cause up and lehters will be rolling in. Frea K or you'lll get a lot more male than you're used to getting. Cud u handle that? Pretty big threht, isn't it?

Dahrn right it is.

Strernly urs,

The Alpha-Bits Wihzard

Why Circus Performers Make Perfect Criminals

by Peter DiChellis

The Lion Tamer knows how to get past the guard dog.
Tightrope Walkers are nimble second-story burglars.
The Bearded Lady confuses eyewitnesses.
When cops frisk the Sword Swallower, they never find a weapon.
Midgets are the perfect height to work as pickpockets.
You can't charge the Jugglers with possession because they don't hold anything long enough.
The Human Cannonball always makes a quick getaway.
If the Mimes get caught, they won't say nothin' to nobody.
The Ringmaster is the brain behind the operation. The Strong Man provides the muscle.
There's plenty of room to hide loot in an Elephant's trunk.
Acrobats are trained to jump anything, even bail.
The Clowns look friendly. (Except to Coulrophobes. Google it.)
The Fire Eater burns any evidence.
The Magician makes the cops disappear.
And every couple of months this clever freak show packs up and travels to another town.

Freaking Out in Bangkok

by Andrew West

Overcast skies cover Bangkok in a sticky blanket, like in Sydney after a summer shower. But here my face phosphoresces with incandescent sweat stimulated by thoughts pouring out of my mind, not smothered by the stifling atmosphere of comfortable familiarity. I'm standing on Surawong Road at the top of Soi Taniya on the edge of Bangkok's Patpong district, a porous sponge for tourists who come from around the globe to be absorbed into its go-go bars and ping-pong shows. I've come to scour this street because I want to write about something new to me for this contribution you are now reading, and even after nine years of living in this city, I've never set foot here. I stare down the receding street. Bars line both sides, catering for Japanese. The freakish crowd and cars coalesce as randomly shuffled dots, set against a backdrop of dark vertical buildings illuminated by irregular blocks of square, round and rectangular colours, red and yellow lights contrasting against grimy concrete façades. The syncopating scene fluxes as groups of half-drunk middle-aged Japanese businessmen flow along the sides of the road between scores of slender Thai woman sitting outside the partitioned bars, calling out to them in staccato Japanese. One moment it's almost quiet and subdued, the next it's loud and even intense. The whole milieu animates as if responding to the beat of a discordant drum, breaking up the groups who step diagonally across the street, before reforming again. It's an immense abstract painting. A Kandinsky or Mondrian, but with a Toulouse-Lautrec twist. I'm touching the edge of the frame, but want to step into the composition. To be the painter, not just the observer—NO!—*to be the paint*. I take my first steps along the pavement into Soi Taniya and become myself, a viscous creation of colours and shapes brushed onto canvas, until disappearing into the vanishing point.

Swedish Fish

by Joseph S. Pete

The pearled woman from marketing cast a handful of candy like a gambler casting dice.

She filled the center table at the newsroom with sweets like Sour Patch, Nestle Crunch, and Swedish Fish, which was billed unironically as a "fat-free food." They skittered across the table then settled into a cornucopia there for the grabbing.

The svelte but perpetually hungry digital producer in the Oxford shirt and stone-washed jeans dashed over, and combed through the pile for the best stuff.

"Goddamned marketing talk," the health reporter said. "You should never eat anything in packaging, because that means it's processed. At most it should have a sticker. If it's got nutritional information on the package, it wasn't nutritional in the first place."

"Well, Christ," the arts reporter said while munching on the candy. "It's not the healthiest stuff. Well, the whole world's not healthy. No one's got all the answers."

Only a few O Henry! bars were left.

The arts reporter felt like a freak, an outcast, stuffing his face with the emptiest of calories while the whole world burned. Another writer, the seemingly appropriately named Steve Almond, who penned "Candyfreak," made such indulgences seem like a stylized delight more than a decade ago, though it felt quaint in an age of superfoods like steamed kale. A far cry from Almond Joy.

The arts reporter, who had been fat his whole life and was probably still considered pudgy now, knew what it was like to really be a freak.

It wasn't something aesthetically twee or hip to be celebrated in a Todd Solondz movie or a Frank Zappa song. Being a freak was an ugly, grungy, pathetic slog through social ostracism and alienation. It was a thousand nights alone pining aimlessly for any attention you could get, however far-fetched and imaginary. It was being scared that someone might see you at a Chinese restaurant, that someone might laugh at you at a cross country meet 60 miles from home. It was utter despairing hopelessness, the kind of misery where the thought of suicide seemed more comfortable than a family Thanksgiving gathering with as much mashed potatoes and sugar-sweet cranberry sauce as it would take to comfort anyone. Being a freak sucked.

Nothing could change that.

People treated you like garbage. Maybe twenty years later plodding around alone and suffering through jock derision gets idealized, but in the short term it's abuse. It's hardly endurable.

You were born with the metabolism you were born with and your heart's not filled with hate and you deserve some goddamned Swedish Fish every once in awhile without the hammer of judgment raining down on you.

Being a freak is being alone, and drowning yourself, whether in cheap beer, slapdash zines or the delusion that someday everything will be better.

The Kid Does His Father a Solid

by Paul Beckman

Do I ask much from you? Anything? Do I ask anything from you? Anything at all?

"Are you talking to me, Dad?"

"You're the only other person in the room."

"Dad, you ask a lot from me."

"What?"

"Take out the garbage. Get good grades. Pick me up from work. It's always something."

"You schmuck, do I ever ask big things from you? No. I don't."

"Right Dad, so what's your point?

"I need you to do something for me and I don't want you to question it or fuck it up or tell your friends—in fact you can't tell anyone."

"Okay. Let's hear, and don't worry, I won't let you down."

"The carnival going on in the empty field between the church and the big box liquor emporium?"

"I was planning to go tonight."

"Go where? Which one?"

"The carnival."

"Perfect. At exactly eight o'clock I want you on the Ferris wheel."

"I was supposed to meet friends at the Mystery Tent to see the Freaks at eight."

"Change to the Ferris Wheel and all go on separate cars."

"Then?"

"I want you to pull a seat pin that will unhinge the rocker you're in and you'll tumble to the ground."

"Do you want me to fall head first or on my back?"

"You won't be high up and since you know this is going to happen you'll be able to grab on to the metal of the wheel."

"That's it?"

"No. I want you screaming and kicking up a fuss even though you'll be safe."

"And what are you going to do? Are you going to come to my rescue?"

"I'll be robbing the ticket booth."

"What the hell are you going to do with the tickets you rob?"

"I'm going to steal the money, you putz, not the fucking tickets. Geez."

"Dad, you're not a robber. You're a used car salesman."

"Not much difference."

"When can I come down?"

"The fire station will probably send a hook and ladder to get you."

"Probably? Then what?"

"We're going to sue the carnival and that'll be your college tuition."

"Why don't I just join the Army infantry and get it over with?"

"Trust me, this is going to be clean and easy."

"What about Mom?"

"Mom's totally on board with this but insists we never speak about it in her presence."

"Just one question, Dad."

"I told you no questions."

"Just one."

"Make it snappy—I've got to get my nap in."

"Why this?"

"Your mother has gambled away our life savings and stolen money from her company and we need to pay it back before she's caught and goes up the river."

"Mom doesn't even go to bingo or say gosh darn."

"That's why we can't mention it. She'd die of embarrassment if you knew."

"When are you going to show me about the bolt?"

"After I get up from my nap."

"You sure I'll be okay?"

"Don't worry. It's like falling off a log."

Robot Lover

by Diana Grove

My robot lover stared out of the bedroom window looking pensive.

"Come back to bed baby."

He turned to me and smiled. I loved that smile. My robot was designed to look just like my husband. Well how my husband looked fifteen years ago when he was in his prime. He died four years ago. Brain tumour.

He lowered himself onto the bed and I ran my hands along his broad shoulders. Jack's artificial skin was soft and supple to the touch just like human skin, and nanobots kept it warm. Jack cost a fortune but he was worth it.

We went out for dinner last night. Jack doesn't eat obviously, but it's nice to go out as a couple and do normal couple things. We went to my favourite Korean restaurant and I caught the train home by myself afterwards because Jack wanted to go to an ACTivate meeting. He's become interested in robot politics.

*

Jack kissed me deeply then pulled away looking serious.

"Something happened last night ... I was followed from the station after I left you."

"What? Why didn't you tell me?"

"You were sleeping when I got home."

"Are you ok?" I asked, unable to see any damage.

"I'm fine."

Jack looked away and a swirling ball of fear grew in my stomach.

"Two men came up behind me. They shoved me and said awful things."

"What kind of things?"

"You know. The usual stuff bot-haters say. Talking vibrator. Sexslave. Hotbot freak."

"Bastards."

"I got angry. I told them robots don't have to put up with insults or injustice. Then one of them punched me. I should have run. I was a block from the meeting hall. But instead I retaliated."

I was stunned. Robots were never violent.

"I threw the one who punched me into a wall and when the other one came at me I snapped his neck."

"Oh Jesus."

"They're both dead."

We sat in silence until the intercom buzzed. The wall screen showed two police officers with their weapons drawn at the front door.

Jack held my hands in his and said, "I need you to do something for me, Grace."

"What?" I said in a whisper.

"Press reset. Then there'll be no data for them to find."

"But you'll be gone. Erased," I said, crying.

"They know I was there," he said. Of course. All robots have locators. "But without my data they can't prove anything. There were no witnesses. *Please.* I don't want you to suffer for my crime. I don't want people raking through my memories and hurting you with them … Sullying *us.*"

I believed Jack truly loved me, so I did what he asked and I was charged with obstruction of justice. In prison I realised it wasn't me Jack wanted to protect; it was ACTivate. He didn't want his actions to hurt the nascent robot rights movement. He deceived me because he couldn't escape capture or reset himself. It hurt, but I still missed him.

The Respect They Deserve

by Jennifer Rose

Rubin's a freak of nature. He was born that way, skinny and underfed. The doctors yanked him out of the starvation cell that was his mother's womb.

It was worse for her. What had she done to deserve this? The cut was deeper than a C-section. She had done all the right things a pregnant woman does these days – not eating this or that, not drinking a whole lot of other stuff. So, why her?

Now she was deprived of the joys of breast feeding – the agony of sore and cracked nipples, the anxiety of wondering why he wasn't attaching properly, the drug-like euphoria of mother and child at one with milk and each other.

The doctors took blood samples from her, Rubin and hubby and sent them overseas. It was a genetic puzzle to the doctors and researchers as to why the child had been born this way. Truly a freak event had brought him to her. What was it – one in how many millions?

Her mum told her it couldn't happen to a more suitable person. She loved Rubin and she was organised and smart enough to cope with him.

The mother of a freak is an awesome sight to behold. Watch out kindys, schools, teachers and anyone else who backs away from treating her freak with the respect he or she deserves. Scary.

Awesome.

200 North Willow Street

by Ben Pitts

My grandpa told me a story as we finished working on the Chevy. Tools slid and bolts clanked—a silver puddle beside his elbow bent into the rust of the truck's belly. He said the old folks were a couple of freaks with strange habits. The kind that hung up their laundry all year long. The type who turned the lights off when neighbors would knock on the door with misplaced mail. That's why no one knew they were gone until their kids went looking for them. It was 12pm on a Sunday when an untucked dress shirt tapped on Grandpa's door and asked if he had seen his dad. It had been almost three weeks since phone calls went unanswered. "I told 'em I hadn't seen a trace of them." Weeks turned to months. No movement at all from the strange people three doors down. "Curiosity can grind on you like a belt-sander. I needed to see inside that house." The window was easy to pry open. In the glow of his flashlight the walls were holding their breath. Toast crumbs on the counter. Clocks scraping in the dark for no one. On an end-table, endless pictures of grandkids framed and precise. "It was like they left for work, but never came home." The police said they'd check things out. The yellow caution tape didn't stop the neighborhood from forming a mob and watch a plastic-wrapped couch and two recliners carried into trucks and driven away. Rumors of kidnapping became whispers of murder until the house was emptied and fresh paint covered every glimpse of those two. "That was about ten years ago, but I can still feel the inside of that house. That kind of quiet sticks with you." He slid out from under the truck and we packed up the tools. "What do you think happened to them?" A pause. "Maybe they just wanted to leave." I pictured a red truck gliding to the sun. His hand in hers, into the unknown.

Outcast

by Melisa Quigley

I see your abhorrence when I walk past
I am not a freak, grotesque, weird or odd
I suffer from depression and anxiety
Made to feel a misfit in my own society
But in lots of ways I am just like you
Please don't judge me
The birthmark on my face shouldn't define me

Magpie

by Glen Donaldson

Magpie had always been so very obviously different.

The children at his new school liked to cruelly joke he was an introduced species. Some of the more scientifically minded twelve-year olds in his class had even gone so far as to 'classify' him as the huffy hybrid. By anyone's definition, his was indeed a most rare skin pigmentation disorder. It wasn't every day people got to see someone sporting black arms, white legs and a vertically symmetrical two-toned face.

In the end, Magpie did what any magpie would do – he swooped and attacked. From that day on his new nickname "Butcherbird" didn't earn him any more friends, but did, at least in the playground, afford him a portion more respect.

Alert

by Dianne Turner

Wild like a tasered tiger
she growled words
they lingered on her lip ready to twist,
        turn and backflip
brown eyes wide, black with hurt
there was no calming her even with the
        creation of music
her way forward was not to forget
"I won't forget, not his cruelty!" she yelled.
        "I won't go in there, I won't go in there;"
she faltered, tears were close but she would
        determine their freefall
not here not this day

She was anger and rage swirling with unseen injuries
and he standing in line smiling
"You freak, no wonder you're in the
        special ed," he snickered
she kicked him, his bag and he ran
        into the classroom laughing
"I won't go in there, no music, no laughter,
        not with him, not with his cruelty."

and yet, with just as assured determination,
        she slipped in through the door
sat quietly on the edge of her imagination
cruelty of another keeping all her senses on alert
too young, I thought sadly
for such sentry feelings

White Ink

by Samantha Armatys

There is a vagina in a box by the bed. Not mine, I didn't mean to see it, but I can't unsee it now. The ceramic form wrapped in a tea towel — white smooth surfaces usually reserved for the finest cuisine. I wonder who the model was or whether the shape was imagined like some shrine. I don't touch it. I put the box in my handbag, the desire to display the contents on a shelf overwhelming. How strange life can be sometimes.

I didn't come here like some kind of freak to steal artificial genitalia from a stranger. Sitting on a worn blanket printed with the face of a roaring tiger, I am struggling to remember why I came at all. The bed isn't mine — the room juts off a hallway stinking of age. Many closed doors. Something tells me that I might be in a retirement home — the kind that fills spare rooms with young people who can't pay normal rent. The truth written in the hallway — a sideboard draped with lace doilies — the way that the Yellow Pages is tattered from actually being used — the way that there is a bit of death in the air.

"I didn't think you were coming," he said when he opened the door.

I haven't done this before, but I guess you're supposed to expect some discrepancy from the advertisement. It's probably safer to expect nothing at all. The seduction only works if you're charmed by sadness or the chaos of the unknown.

"Wait here," he goes to get a CD from his car.

There is a song for this occasion that I have not yet heard. My heart beats faster left alone in an unfamiliar room, reveling in the unspoken trespasses of touching things that don't belong to me. That's when I find the box. We don't speak after that. I lay back into the snarling teeth, stiff with uncertainty. The music from the crackling speakers is loud and aggressive – a rapper with ugly words.

I shake my head, no; this soundtrack isn't mine. I wriggle away from the touch, the grasping hands, the eye contact, the words, the thoughts, the being there at all. I don't say sorry. I adjust my shirt, pick up my bag and close the door – past the decaying paper and lace – sucking in the outside air, youthful, alive.

In the dim afternoon light I drive until the moment is as distant as it was before – fantasy or a memory, who knows? Both just thoughts sold differently. At home I take the box from my handbag. I feel the weight for a moment before removing the lid. The vagina looks up at me with a story written in white ink. I read the words with my hands. I turn the shape over, admiring the symmetry. It belongs to me now. I place my new object on the shelf, and smile.

A Baby on Board

by Em Koenig

A baby on board
A light aircraft will not
Wear a seatbelt and screams.

The bottle is empty and
Uncomfortable – the mothers
In the space are thinking
It too.
The shadows are limp and
Burning, the baby on board
Refuses to wear a seatbelt – no smoking
On board the aircraft.
   Would you like anything
 from the menu?

The baby refuses its safety
Restraint is uncomfortable
The hostess is thinking
It too.

The baby is not in the
Aircraft, thinks the mother
As she slips through the
Safety and into
A puddle.

A mother on board a light aircraft
Will not wear a seatbelt,
Will not be restrained, will not
Feel uncomfortable.
The bottle is empty,
Would you like anything
          From the menu?

Nobody Here But Us Chickens

by Andrew Stancek

"Truth," Mirko says to Duro, "is always relative." He pulls the chicken's head through the bottom of the killing cone, cuts behind where the tendon attaches for the beak and tongue. He severs the jugular vein and carotid artery, slices, pulls the head down and allows the blood to drain. "Suppose I was convinced that fresh chicken blood brings on superpowers; I drank some of the magic elixir and then ran up the stairs, climbed on the roof, and in the hospital told you that I did fly. While your truth would be that I consumed three uppers too many, mine would be that once out of traction I'd return to this amazing job with magical chicken blood, and stunning Natasha," he bows across the cutting floor and Natasha rolls her eyes, "would agree to a hot date, because a man with one superpower might have another, more pleasing one."

Mirko scalds the chicken but Duro, instead of keeping up, is not ready for the removal of the feathers and has stopped working next to the scalding tank, ready to strangle his friend. He is madly, hopelessly in love with Natasha.

Duro clutches his pinning knife, aims it as if to throw at Mirko. "Your ignorance is only exceeded by your Philosophy 101 pretentiousness. The idiotic story only proves the absolute truth of that, not a relative one. If you combined the superpowers of Superman with those of the Wizard of Oz and Mephistopheles, Natasha would not touch you. Another absolute truth. Go ahead, drink some fresh chicken blood, turn into an even more grotesque freakazoid. Since you are careless with your knife like that, you'll also cut off a hand, and Natasha and I will cackle watching your blood seep out. Once you finish twitching, Natasha will cut off a chicken head, then cut off yours and we'll ride into the sunset on my motorcycle."

Mirko and Natasha laugh. Natasha cuts off a chicken head, slits the skin and opens it up to the breast bone. She frees and removes the entrails, washes the bird and herself. It is her last day on this last day of the summer. She's finished at Schmidt's. Next week her term at film school begins. "Both of you are idiots, destined to remain chicken-cutters forever, or more likely, until you maim yourselves. I still won't go out with either of you. But tonight the Cinematheque is showing the Boris Karloff Frankenstein and if you two meet me in front, no blood on hands, shirts or in vials, I may sit with you, even without superpowers. And that is *my* truth, both relative and absolute."

Mirko slaps Duro a high-five. Behind them a headless chicken squawks, lifts off and glides around the room in mid-air without anyone noticing. Having circled, it resumes its rightful place.

Something real

by Kathryn Lee

God, of all the people I have to see now. Crap. I just want to get some bananas and go home. And there's the big freak, standing outside the front of my supermarket.

Why did I get involved with him?

In the daylight, he looks like just some old guy with a stomach and cargo shorts, not the man in the suit on our blind date who sat back and asked if I was wild.

I avoided answering that question, but it lurked in my head for the rest of the year.

Wild?

Maybe I could be wild with the right person.

Then his reply to my casual happy new year text set the wild times rolling.

God, I guess these bananas will have to do. What else do I need?

Sitting outside the pub, he teased me about my fancy vocabulary and honed into my word snobbery, throwing lots of *awesomes* into his talk. But later on, after the wine, out came this stare of a man who had been in the wilderness too long. Asking me pedestrian questions about whether I liked to perform various acts.

It was like a job interview. Yet I went back for more.

Then the next time, after the champagne, he squawked at me like a chicken when I turned down his suggestion we go to a swingers' club, saying he thought real writers wanted experience.

I wanted to say, I've had enough experience. I want something real. But I just let him squawk at me some more.

I should get something nice to eat for lunch, like some smoked salmon.

And in the dark, his words were those of a schoolboy as he skipped most of the preliminaries.

And no interest, when I made suggestions.

Such wild times.

And yet I went back for more.

I need some dark chocolate.

I should have shouted something out the front, like, *Hey Stefan, still talking about selling your business?*

At times, he would forget the upkeep of his man about town demeanour and let out all his worries. Always the same ones. Never any change.

And he just sat there in the mornings in his singlet and boxers refuelling on cordial and Monte Carlo biscuits.

And still I kept texting.

Jesus, put the chocolate back.

But sometimes I see something, like that Leunig cartoon, and I think he's the only person who could find the words to articulate what it is really saying.

Maybe I should talk to him.

For God's sake, put the chocolate back. He was barely functioning, and there's a story in there about a man who spends his working life unpicking others' troubles, while trapped within his own.

But you're the bigger freak. There's another story in there about the woman who sees the bad times ahead and can't help but let them unroll.

So Stefan, I'm writing you off as a bad experience. But I guess I should also thank you for showing me something real.

Blue Lady

by Irene Buckler

A tear rolls down her cheek when she catches a glimpse of her reflection in the small mirror on the sun visor as she drives. She is a freak – an abstract portrait, facial features rearranged and peculiarly off-centre. Her broken nose is crooked and her right eye nestles oddly in its broken eye socket, sitting lower than her left. Her mouth skews downwards, anchored to the end of a jagged scar that runs diagonally from her ear through her cheek to her chin. Smiling is impossible.

She has always blamed herself for the beatings, believing she somehow triggers the violence, but the truth is that he cannot control his demons and he punishes her for his weakness. She knows that now.

Their car hugs the corners of the deserted road. She is driving at breakneck speed as he sleeps it off in the passenger seat beside her. He is as handsome as ever, but she knows they are the same, both damaged beyond repair.

He barely stirs when she drives their car over the cliff, but she is smiling on the inside.

I Toast
a Most Solemn Occasion:

by Ruth Sabath Rosenthal

mass destruction, like what I've seen blasted
on TV and plastered all over newspapers. *My* weapon,
my father's gun. I'll smuggle it into school,
     under heavy denim,
along with a shit-load of bullets, and fire at
     anyone I please —
my free arm raised in glory, both of theirs,
     in useless protection.
Each Mother's daughter & son I shoot, my retribution
     for being
called *Freak*. And freak-show that I plan,
     I intend on being
the one and only kid left standing, by the time
     I'm taken down.

Faulty Tan Line

by Kristina England

It happened as such.

I went on a two-hour sail that turned into a four and a half hour trip. As I was only on the local lake and anticipating a less lengthy presence under the sun, I burned as my mostly Irish and Swedish skin screamed at me, my Syrian widow's peak merely for show.

I emerged a week later in my bathing suit with a faulty tan, ready to head to the beach, my legs dark up until the point above my knees, then the color of natural stockings.

"Jesus, Krissy," a friend said.

"I know, I know," I replied, almost calling myself a freak, but biting back the word as it still stung like a hot branding iron from my awkward high school days of crooked smiles and a long face the boys called "monkey."

I drove an hour and a half with two friends to a beach in Connecticut without another word about the mismatched elephant in the room. We met up with several other friends who all nodded to my legs and said, "ouch."

An hour later, I braved the quasi warm water and reemerged cool and happy. I headed for my blanket, but before I could get there, a woman called out from my right. "Giiiirl, those are some uneven tan lines. You need a class on proper balance."

I could feel several nearby beachgoers turn towards me like a boat that had shifted in the wind. I faced her and laughed playfully. "I know, right."

"Seriously, what were you thinking," the stranger said, lying on her belly, her cleavage half exposed, her body round and heavy, but knowingly carried with much more gravitas than mine.

"I'm a sailor. It's a casualty of the role."

She looked at me as if I was weirder than before. I smiled, waved goodbye and headed towards my blanket. A friend's four-year old daughter followed behind, looking confused. I heard the woman say loudly. "I won't forget her. She's an example of what not to do, huh."

My friend's daughter looked up at me. There was so much I wanted to say to her, to explain bullying, body shaming, and everything in between. I wanted to turn to that woman and tell her to apologize, tell her how much her words stung than my overbaked epidermis.

Instead, I walked in silence, my shoulders slouched. I spent the rest of the day trying to position myself just right, as if I could even things out, but my skin throbbed, the redness brighter, radiating a heat I could not simply soothe with aloe.

Pea Coat

by Anne E. Weisgerber

She stepped up to the National Airlines ticket desk and, man, she was thirsty. Beep boop everybody's phone pinged delayed departure chimes.

She hadn't even sat down before approaching the gate. She said hi and smiled at the average-looking agent. He perked up pretty fast. Oh, she was thirsty. Minutes earlier I had watched her warmly hug her boyfriend at the curb, but now, at check-in, she was flirting hard; I caught myself Michael-Jackson-popcorn-giffing.

And by the way: LAX. And by the way: my lucky pea coat was in the bag National lost three days ago.

On my Galaxy, there's a dog all over the *Russian Times* website. Some kind of Sasquatch dog eating luggage and window seats. I trust *RT*. Dog prolly tore this National Air terminal down the middle and duck-dropped it two different places, like gnawed nasty slippers on the tarmac.

That explained why National Air spread across two gross terminals. There were dog prints all over the mess. People were dressed like there were zero fucks. But then: Thirsty sashayed over my way, had a seat. She took a sip of me.

She said: "So look at this."

She swiped through pictures of what looked like a metal-shop project, but I realized it's the framework of an airplane seat with zero upholstery. In one photo, I recognized ports and jacks and the silver call button on what must be two fold-up arms. "Did you take that?"

"My last National flight should have been decommissioned," Thirsty peeked from behind her shades. "It was like: was that the first Airbus ever?"

What's her angle? What's she hiding?

She said, "It's that dog."

Coincidentally, Average Agent hopped on the intercom and said: "We are going to give you complimentary noisemakers. We are going to give you baseball bats. We are going to give you two-by-fours. There is no need to push. We have plenty."

I noted a wheelie garbage can nearby, filled with broken hockey sticks.

And everybody's phone went beep boop buzz, and a map of the terminal opened on every Galaxy, our inbound plane approached Gate 6 like some Über arcade Asteroid. Thirsty paced with her rollerbag.

"I'm going to give a signal," Average Agent said, as a silver airbus rolled in from the west, shining like a food truck, "and you are going to swing those sticks, people."

The plane taxied up, coupled up with the gangplank. Thirsty sashayed over to get a better view from the window wall. Average Agent said 3. 2. 1!

Thirsty jumped; she ran around in a circle first then leapt into the sky, gone through that glass like Herman Munster, and all our gate-checks and in-flight Dewar's and flotation devices poured out of her mouth. My lucky pea coat, too. Oh hell yes.

Average Agent helped me into my sleeves.

Widow

by Tina Barry

He suggested they meet in a rotating bar for a drink. "After that," he said, "We'll see."

"We'll see," bothered her. We'll see what? If he'd want her?

The date hadn't been her idea. "Go," her friend Natalie had said. "You need it."

Hair blown out, legs waxed; she waited on a barstool. A gin and tonic, then another, produced kind thoughts: the bartender's "New in town?" Funny! The tourists on the dance floor grooving to "Super Freak": charming. And didn't the mirrored column behind the bar reflect lovely, dappled light? A spot of it rested on her cheekbone.

That must be him, she thought. He was muscular; Natalie got that right. Was his hair dirty or too much mousse? And he kissed her cheek. A nice gesture. She was fine with the litchi martini he ordered. Really.

"What's that?" Oh yes, she knew he was divorced. So sorry to hear it.

"Messy," he said, shrugging.

"Me? Yes, a widow. A widow for one year." Did he recognize the title? John Irving? There's a glimmer of something. But no, no. And why should he know Irving's book? Her husband had hated Irving, and her defending the author's early work (she loved the bears!) had grown old.

"He's good for one thing," Natalie had said. Maybe her friend was right about this date. Maybe the earth had turned on its axis offering her this small token.

On the dance floor, he smelled limey, like her gin and tonic. Not a disagreeable scent. Over his shoulder, beyond the wall of windows, the city moved in a slow circle: amber lights blinked in gray spires; a thumbnail-sized plane drifted past then disappeared.

The music slowed. He pulled her closer. Yes, she thought. It had been too long since a man touched her. Yes, because that hand, warm on the small of her back, brought comfort. Yes, because a year is a long time to be a widow.

Peachy Head

by Mark Govier

2016

The infamous Peachy Head suicide jump chalk cliff towers some 300 metres above a jagged, rock-strewn beach.

We climb down to the Café, cited in all good alternate travel guides. The white building nearby is marked 'Undertakers'.

I decide to pay extra, to get a good seat.

Tim, my fellow traveller, smiles. 'Nice choice,' he says, 'we can see everything from here.'

A waiter, dressed from head to foot in blood-red, strolls over to our table.

'Would you like a drink first, sirs?'

'We'll have the special rice wine,' we say.

'What sort of flavours, sirs?'

Tim and I laugh. 'Apricot,' we reply, together.

The waiter returns with our drinks.

Tim orders duck rice, I order chicken rice.

'Do you want any dessert, sirs?'

No, we say, but we'll definitely have another drink.

'When's the Jumping supposed to start?' asks Tim, tucking into his duck.

It's nearly 1:00 PM. 'About an hour,' I reply.

By now, the Café is standing room only.

It's a pleasant day, the sun shines, waves lap rocks, a light breeze wafts.

Tim removes a pack of Ritalin-Extra from his shirt pocket. There's no rice wine left in the carafe, so we swallow another.

At 1:45, an announcement is made, in five languages.

'At 2:00 PM precisely, the Peachy Head Beach will be closed. No customers will be allowed to leave until 4:00 PM. If you do not wish to remain, please leave the area now. Staff will assist anyone with mobility or other health problems walking up the Chalk Steps.'

No one leaves the Café.

As 2:00 PM arrives, all conversation ends. The Program says first Jumper is a 32-year old man. In anticipation, we remove our photo-binoculars, like everyone else, look up.

'This freak does look doped,' whispers Tim.

I focus on the Jumper's face. Tim's right. We snap shots. The State Social Worker appears, a woman dressed in black. She approaches the Jumper, to make the 'last appeal'. The man ignores her, jumps, is torn to pieces on the rocks.

'What's next?' asks Tim.

I check the program. 'It's an old woman, at 2:15.'

'I'm going to the bar, want one?'

I do. Tim returns, just in time. This Jumper looks 70. The State Social Worker re-appears, the freak jumps. Splat!

By 3:30, Tim's staring vacantly into space.

'The Undertakers come soon,' I say, 'could be interesting.'

By 4:00 PM Jumping finishes. The Café doors open. A few spectators have had enough. They amble towards the Steps, talking loudly. The Undertakers emerge from the white building. They're dressed in white, carry electric saws, large white plastic cartons.

'Do they separate them?' I ask Tim.

'Don't know,' he replies, snapping more shots, 'check the guidebook.'

'It says *the Jumpers' remains are collected together, cremated together, strewn together, in the Suicides Garden at the local Council cemetery.*'

The train rockets back to the Traveller's Getaway.

'Got some great shots,' we say together, popping another Ritalin-Extra.

Koo Laid

by Catfish McDaris

I've written on all kinds of things. One time I was grocery shopping with my lady and the muse grabbed me by the balls. I always keep a lucky pen and a sheet of paper in my pocket, well I filled up the paper. People were looking at me like I was a total freak. My lady had left me in the aisle, she's used to my ways. I grabbed a Koolaid box and emptied out all the packets and started writing on the box. I looked up and two store employees were frowning at me, I kept writing. I told them I'd buy all the Koolaid and I started writing on the packets. My lady finished her shopping, she just shook her head when I finally came out of my freak trance.

The Peacock and the Poodle

by Mark Hudson

I went to Brookfield zoo in Chicago with a
friend this summer. Brookfield Zoo has a lot of
peacocks. Talk about a unique-looking creature!
The creator has set the peacock up with a colorful
display of feathers, a perfect excuse to show off,
and have a big ego. But when you think of it,
what is the peacock but a "freak of nature?"
    When we saw the peacock at the zoo,
a group of grade-school children on a field
trip were "ruffling the peacock's feathers."
They were coming close and provoking it,
and he was flapping his wings, as if to
say, "This means war."
    My sister operates a dog shelter out of
her basement, in association
with the dog shelter.
    "I've got just the dog for you,"
my sister said. "There is a poodle that nobody
wants, and it has messed up teeth, but I think
she has a sweet personality."
    To me, poodles are dogs for old ladies.
Finally, one night I called, lacking appreciation,
and said, "Sorry, but I don't need a

poodle. Poodles are for old ladies. I need a
real man's dog!" and hung up.

Shortly after that, my sister called and said,
"I'm glad you called, because the poodle got
sold today, and I thought you'd be disappointed."

In all fairness, I said, "My main concern
was that the creature find a home." And meant it.

A week later, my sister called, and said,
"The poodle was returned. Would you like
to take it after all?"

So I replied, "I don't think I can handle a dog
right now."

But lately, I've been feeling like the poodle.
I even had to have a tooth extracted at age forty-five.
Living on my own, I'm bombarded by "freaky voices."
One person in high school nicknamed me "freak,"
once, but that is a separate poem for another venue.

Not to sound religious, but Jesus said,
"Whatever you do for the least of these, you
have done for me." I try to keep that in mind,
because I was once referred to by a friend as
"the bottom of the barrel." (Actually he was,
but you didn't hear it from me.) The person
who is the worst freak on earth could become
beautiful in heaven, and the most beautiful creature
on Earth could become an eternal monster in
the world down below. At least that's what I've
heard. But I think it would benefit us all if we
were a little less critical of one other, a bit
more encouraging. It's like the beautiful woman
who is a knockout, with one unsightly birth
mark on her neck. They say beauty is on the

inside. And when I had a colonoscopy, I
was supposed to be knocked out, but I wasn't.
So I saw on the screens what my insides
look like. And guess what, people?
I'm full of shit!

Pearl

by Donna Krause

A true descendant of "WOODSTOCK".
Long flowing hair braided up tight
Rolled up with joints
Ready to be smoked
Savored by her clan
A weekend warrior
Choosing the right fix
Cocaine detached her from reality
While fuzzy mushrooms
Took her for a wild
Mystical ride
Pearl never dreamed
It could have caused her demise
Left the drug scene behind
To get hitched
Surrounded by her three children, now
Each healthy, an unspoken relief
Pearl works the soil
Paints her bamboo
Magic garden so tall and plush
A burst of colors
Sweet violet, rose petal pink, sunny yellow
And eye-popping red

One floated away from the natural perfume
Pearl gave those gifts to the earth.
Birds that soared above her soothed her
As she named each one
They sang to her sweetly, out back on her porch
Pearl's generosity abounds
Brought food for the sick
And a dose of her laughter
Our friendship was deep
What a fun companion!
Knew how to party
Got high on life!
My gift was receiving some of her strength
To carry on in this life…

Our Sub-Generation

by John Lambremont, Sr.

We were just too young
to be hippies, born at the tail end
of the baby boomers. Hippies
we found to be boring
and annoying.

We came to age in the face
of horrific violence at home
and abroad: war, rioting,
and assassinations. Being
the first kids to view it
over breakfast on T.V.
numbed our sensibilities.

We did not take drugs
to seek enlightenment
or for adventure; we took them
to get drunk and fucked up,
bombed out of our skulls,
and not caring.

We were the first head bangers,
invented the mosh pit,
and wore grunge; tee shirt,
flannel shirt unbuttoned,
straight-leg blue jeans,
and sneakers; twenty years
before the Northwest grungers.

To us, our music was everything:
we watched rock-n-roll become RAWK,
ushered in heavy metal.
Our box guitars were our constant
companions, and we jammed
incessantly in garages
and at bus stops.

We despised disco with a passion,
considered The Outlaws clod-hoppers,
and found some hope in punk.
We attended concerts, but not rallies,
as politics and achievement
were for ass-kissers and fools.

We were classic underachievers
who never gave a shit, too lazy
and indifferent to look up "nihilist."

We were The Freaks.

Sleeping Beauty Doesn't Freak

by Lucy M. Logsdon

Regarding sleep: I've given up.
Once upon a time, I napped unguarded:
legs wide open, drool. That's how
she found me—arms flung slackly.
No ambition. Except to sleep.
She watched, tapped her keypad—
a prototypical black cloud gathered,
tazered me with lightning. My brain
sizzled; frontal lobes flashed.
I was now wired to write.
Exactly what she wanted.
Always when she wanted.
Between our conferences,
I slumped to the floor. My witch,
my teacher, my poetry, She brought
all the dark books. Plath. Sexton.
Macdonald. Wakowski. Rich.
Seminars must stop; student too fragile—
she wrote the Dean. Perhaps she loved me.
Maybe I was the only reflection she could get.
Static promise, flawed perfection.
Too timid for revision, I refused
to change the lines. She fed me fruit,

whispered: *the apple doesn't fall far
from the tree.* I stayed until some wretch
added a new plot twist: *soon she'll forget
everything she's ever known.*
Her memory drained so fast,
hemorrhaged poems, theories,
sonnets, villanelles, sestinas stained
my nightgown for years.
The witch was dead.
If I had the poison, I would kill
to be her apple once more
—so red, ripe, so fallen, forever
at her black-shoed feet.

Digital Music Dude

by Alex Robertson

He didn't have extrasensory powers
Nor a Utility Belt like Bruce Wayne did
Strength was not a forte
And he had no nous for clairvoyance
His lot was being pale and freckly
Whilst his imagination ran away with him

The texts he received were cryptic
Messages from unlisted numbers
"Help me" and "I need to be saved…"
Appear on his phone
Little was his perception
     to know who sent them
A potential admirer who appreciated him?
Who was he to protect someone
From their ultimate demise?

His control lay in his music
The ear buds distracting him
From the world around him
Amazing things happened
When he was wired for sound
Clouds seemed to part
And the sun was a bit brighter
Positivity was the weapon of choice
Not being a superhero
        but someone who could change destiny

He ignored the ruffians around him
He knew they were mean
Shouting "Freak!" and "Creep!" at him
But he never heard them
In his indulgent moments
Whilst listening to Silverchair or Radiohead
In that self-deprecating mood
When Uptown Funk didn't suit…

Adult Adolescence

by Hasen Hull

Oliver developed a tendency to wake up half-mad in the middle of the night, sweaty with the conviction he was wasting his youth, and when he met Kate he found she felt much the same way. They discussed how boring university was (such a bore), revelled in their desire to be able to one day ask "Do you remember when" and expressed shared horror at the prospect of growing old without having really lived.

"So let's travel the world," he said, a little self-consciously, because it was exactly this sort of generic undertaking that the both of them had grown sick of.

"But where would we go?" she asked, genuinely interested, or just playing along.

"Who cares? We'll just *go*." And it was this spontaneity, this complete lack of a plan they latched onto, as proof of what separated them from the herd. They hopped on a plane to Prague ("who's ever been to Prague?" they guessed hopefully), savoured the complimentary soft drinks and subsequently retired to a toilet stall, where they joined the Mile High club above what they wrongfully assumed to be Amsterdam.

Prague was "alright" but this business with the toilet stall was what really caught their attention, and under the right circumstances it was cheaper and more spacious too. They took to back rows of empty cinemas, labyrinthine alleyways that an apprehensive Oliver had to be coaxed down, and park benches that they felt a little guilty about in the moments after, silently envisioning an OAP sitting down the next morning to take in the view.

"But what we really need is to stick it to them," Kate said.

"Them?" Oliver asked.

"The establishment!"

So in love or in lust's mysterious way, Oliver nabbed a key from the staffroom and they found themselves locked inside Lecture Room 1.16, in the highest row of seats, shagging with their clothes still on, their movement inwardly tender and outwardly vitriolic, to prove a point and make a statement that in conspicuous ecstasy they'd altogether lost sight of.

The doorknob rattled and a member of staff let someone in, and they were already down behind the desks, covering their mouths with widened eyes, when the little do-gooder, little Teacher's Pet that he was, took a seat with notebook and pen an entire hour before class.

There was no choice but to stand up, to make themselves known, and in the bemused laughter that followed, in the argument that saw Oliver and Kate storm out, they could see that little Teacher's Pet would tell his friends and tell his followers that he thought the two some kind of freak. But they would carry on elsewhere, out of curious affection and youthful principle, a little more carefully, a little more tiredly, not quite sure if what they were doing was adult or adolescent or somewhere in-between.

Toppin' y'self

by Rob Walker

Can't be an easy thing, but.

Toppin' y'self, I mean… Y'know, suicide.

I was just a schoolkid, like, y'know. Little tacker. Playing with the Messner kids in their backyard when we seen the ambulance pull up in Kitson Avenue. Yeah. "Avenue". Spose ta have trees aren't they? Like *Les Grand Avenues* in Paris. Tree-lined. I can't remember one fuckn tree in Kitson Avenue. Just tiny red-brick Housing Trust homes.

Ronnie lived there. His ol' man worked for Gilbarco makin' petrol pumps for service stations. Pretty funny he couldn't afford a car 'imself, eh? Neither did Wayne's old man next-door. He was as tall as he was skinny. We used to joke that he didn't need a ladder to be a linesman for the Electricity Trust, 'cause he could reach the wires anyway. Sometimes he'd spend all his pay of a Fridy night at the pub and we'd have to show him where he lived. The old memory wasn't so good on Fridy nights…

But we didn't know who lived in the old light grey house. Chris said he thought they were New Australians.

When they brought him out on the stretcher you couldn't see him with the blue sheet over his face. Mrs Messner said we couldn't go and watch, but she went down and when she came back she said he'd gassed himself. My grandpa had been gassed in the First War with somethink called "mustard". That was why one of his lungs was collapsed. I was a bit confused how this could happen in a person's house in Richmond South Australia in the 1960s... Later, back home, Mum explained that he'd turned on the oven without lighting it and put his head in...

I couldn't imagine ever being that sad that you didn't want to wake up. When I was a kid, I mean.

They were fixing up Marion Road at the time – making it wide and modern. Tearing up the old tram tracks so they could fit more cars on, I guess. They put these giant steel water pipes under the road and a man went right in on his back on a kind of stretcher with wheels. And he had welding equitment to seal the seams. I almost shat meself as he disappeared, just fittin' in the pipe, like he was buryin' himself alive under the road. Like putting his head in an oven. But he kept coming out and going back in. I thought he was so brave.

Yard Darts

by Carl 'Papa' Palmer

Wendy tells us ahead of time Harold is king of his yearly yard dart tournament, warns me on how he embarrasses all comers with his backyard bravado.

Judy had mentioned I was a pretty good horseshoe player back in the day, so Wendy's hoping I may be the one to beat her boasting husband at his own game and invites us to their annual summer patio party.

The men gather by the tub filled with cold bottles of beer while the women set the covered tables with massive amounts of food.

As anticipated, after dinner and a couple hours of beer, Harold announces the tournament to begin. Each of us eight men are expected to play and as in the past throw a five dollar entry fee into the pot.

"Let's up the ante this year," Harold smiles. "Ten bucks."

An underhand tossing method is used, same as when pitching horseshoes, however the 12 inch dart is much lighter than the regulation 2 pound 10 ounce horseshoe.

The distance is 35 feet between the two eighteen inch diameter plastic rings instead of the 40 feet between one inch diameter metal stakes measuring 15 inches out of the ground in horseshoes.

Harold's Scoring Rules:

Each player has two darts, either red or blue. Three points are earned for landing each dart inside the ring. One point earned for landing the closest outside the ring if the opponent is not in the ring. Tie throws cancel each other out.

Example: Red lands two in the ring. Blue gets one in and one out. Three points for red. None for the blue.

The game goes to 21 unless one side gets to 11 before the other gets any points, which results in a Skunk.

Our eight names are put in the hat to determine who plays on each of the four two-man teams the first round. Harold puts our names in blocks on his poster paper score board.

Rumor is he has a stack of sheets from every year's past tournament game in his garage.

The four winners of the first round are then put in the hat for the next round of competition of two teams, leaving only one final winning team, Harold and me to go head to head for the final grand championship game.

Before we start, Harold asks loudly if I'd like to take a friendly side bet "just to make things more interesting."

The crowd cheers when I pull out a twenty and say, "But first, let's have another beer."

I drink my beer slow, throw a few practice shots back and forth while Harold plays the crowd.

Walking back I mention that it's getting pretty dark, ask if he has a yard light.

Knowing the distance by heart and playing with home court advantage, Harold could easily throw with his eyes closed and hit the ring consistently.

"Oh, don't worry, it's not that dark. No more stalling. Let's get on with it. This shouldn't take long anyway."

We flip a coin to see who throws first. Harold wins and quickly tosses his two darts, both stick slightly short of the ring. My two land dead center. Six to Zero.

Now my turn to throw first, both darts land in the ring. Harold's two darts go long.

A skunk. I win. Twelve to Zero.

The crowd goes wild. The king is dead.

Long live the king.

That next year when Harold breaks out the Yard Darts the two rings are tied together at the prescribed distance with a rope so they can't be "accidentally nudged" when it starts to get a little dark.

Echo, Echo

by Richie Narvaez

My cubicle is right outside the ladies' room. I do not try to listen, but with the shape of the walls and the vent in the door, I hear the echo of things I am not meant to hear.

I hear gossip, of course, sometimes whispered, sometimes yelled. I learn about everyone in the office. My boss is getting divorced. I did not know that. Suzie in accounting apparently sucks at her job but runs a very good side business out of her cubicle. I even hear about me. Something that sounds like a compliment about my vocabulary.

Every day, a woman from legal likes to sing in there. At 8:30, before the office becomes crowded, and after most people leave, at 6 or 7 p.m. Her voice is lovely, and it's not a pop song or anything, just a series of trills and notes echoing off the tile. A nightingale song.

I tell Bob from IT to come by and listen, and he hears it and says, "Does she sing before or after she flushes?"

She must have heard us giggling because suddenly she stops singing and after that she never sings again.

I did not ask to be seated here. I try to make the best of it. No one looks at me when they come out, maybe because they think I am listening. And I feel bad because I am and can't help it.

I consider standing up as women walk out of the bathroom and pointing to my watch and then looking at them with eyebrow-high disapproval. I think it might be a fun icebreaker. But I never do it. I'd get in trouble.

One day sounds of splashing and loud laughter flow through the vent. This goes on for almost an hour. Then it suddenly stops and four women file out, not looking at me, not looking at each other, not looking at anything. Their clothes are sopping wet.

I wonder what goes on in there. It sounds a lot more interesting than the men's room. In the men's room, Mr. Kelper will have a whole conversation with you while you sit in a stall. He can recognize everyone by their shoes. You don't have to say a thing, he will start talking to you as he enters and keep talking until he leaves.

Months later, my boss tells me that cubicles are being reorganized and I'll be moving to one that is around the corner from a window. I do not mention his divorce.

After that, but before I move to the new space, the nightingale begins singing again. Her trills float high and low. She could be an opera singer. She could sing on stage, in front of hundreds, thousands. I realize then how much I missed her voice.

When she emerges from the bathroom, I stand up and applaud. She snorts at me and calls me a freak.

Too Late and Too Long Ago

by Pádraig Ó Cúana

It's too late and too long ago
I scramble and stuff together
reasons for my slow and targeted persecution
as if it were my responsibility

How could I not have known?
My fault
Everything
Every last little bit is my fault
I cannot bear the burden of a civilisation's suffering
The guilt burns my throat

Surely there must have been some way out
Could I not have been the animal sacrifice
Needed to keep the sun rising each day?
What was I trying to keep safe?
I could have let myself go
Swept myself away in the tide
Given in to my stupid fear of drowning
And drowned like the rest

Perhaps then the vile and violent vermin
would have grown tired of their still and tepid prey

I search for reasons I could have earnt it
Ten years misery

I didn't need to stand out
I was asking for it
If I had kept silent/
Spoken up
Learnt the pop culture/
Not tried to
Behaved more modestly/
Acted more confidently
On and on and on and on

How did I earn my place as a
certified piece of shit?
What in my gestures or words
clarified my position as a
faggot, a pussy, a poser, a psychopath, a try-hard
a wannabe, a cunt, a dipshit, a limp-dick, poofter
wanker, shithead, loner, loser, creep, pervert
arsehole, wimp, nerd, geek, dickhead, dork
ugly, arsewipe, virgin, rapist-looking,
cock-sucker, weirdo, freak
who would die alone?

What gave them that perception?
and how can I learn from my childhood for
        a brighter future?
and as a white, straight, middle-classed, cis-gendered
cis-privileged male
how have I not yet left this behind?

and it's just too late
and too fucking long ago
and maybe those bastards can find their own reasons
these evils needn't mar their souls

he called me a freak

by Stephen House

he called me a freak
when i said
that i had to take off somewhere again
and that i might go anywhere
and not know where
run away like i do
to think things out

i touched his calm bearded face

he called me a freak
when i said
i would take a role in a play
during melbourne winter
learn two hundred pages in six weeks
for a pittance fee and not much more
stay in a dirty room in north fitzroy
and find a café nearby to have somewhere to go

i held his big warm hand in mine

he called me a freak
when i said
i had hooked up with lots of men on grinder
just for the sake of it
for some type of rush
and to fall into online obsessive sex
when horny and wondering
what else to do

we sat still looking out at the beach sunset

he called me a freak
when i said
i was finished with striving for more
and needing the establishment
to validate me and my work
that i would live on what i could
and write poetry
or do a new play now and then

he laughed when i looked into his grey-blue eyes

he called me a freak
when i said
i'd go back to rishikesh
in india
and live a yoga life for a year or so
and not worry about money
or what people think

he sipped his coffee and looked so damn sweet

he called me a freak
when i said
i fell off the wagon
for the first time in ages
and drank twenty drinks over a night
smoked cigarettes
and danced in clubs and got thrown out
like when i was a young and an alcoholic

he leaned across and hugged me when we stopped the car

he's never called me a freak in a bad way
no matter what i said
not once in all of our shared special time
said anything hurtful
about how i am
and the things that i do
and do and do

we walked silently in the rain through the dark city streets

and i never called him anything to hurt either
whatever he said
or did
but we laughed about freak
together once
a couple of freaks we are
hanging out
and how beautiful it is to be a freak
and to find another freak in this crazy life
full of expectations and judgements

we've loved each other for twenty years
and we know we always will

Visitation

by Phillis Ideal

We sat up in bed. It's two o'clock in the morning. Blinding circular flashlight beams probe through the half-pulled shades. Magnified black silhouettes of men's torsos lumber back and forth in the yard. We are in a fishbowl and being invaded.

Someone presses the doorbell long and loud and hard. Gene jumps into his sweatpants and springs to the front door. His voice booms, "Who are you and what the hell do you want?"

"It is the police."

"You stand back. Show me your badge before I open this door."

There are three uniformed policemen and one pushes his badge through the door and says, "A call was made that there is a woman trapped in one of your windows, and we want to know if you can identify her?"

"What? What window?"

Now the police are in the hall, tall and bulging with buckles and belts equipped with handguns, cuffs, flashlights, and batons. I am barefoot in my gown, and Gene has thrown on a shirt. They lead us through our house as if they know the way. Through the large living room windows, more policemen with zigzagging lights are searching the grounds. We circle back to our bedroom, and open the side door that faces the back of my studio. I see a woman, mid-twenties, with flaming dyed cadmium red hair. Half her body and one leg is hanging out of the studio bathroom window. Her white face is spot lit against the night, and I think, *Am I dreaming or seeing an apparition?* Howling in pain, she yelps, "I didn't mean to break in. I was just looking for the little boy."

I walk out of the house and see that the fire truck and ambulance are lining the street. The yard is swarming with police and firemen trying to get her unstuck from the 20" X 20" bathroom window. I trail through my cluttered studio and see her other half, rear end and other leg, straddling a windowsill. In between sobs, she woefully says, "I was just looking for the little boy. I heard him calling."

The ambulance takes her to the hospital, and the police stay and talk to us. They speculate that she was wandering down the back of neighborhood yards, trying doors and found my studio to be open. She went in and locked the door behind her. Disoriented and wanting out of this dark cavernous space, she was drawn toward the light of the full moon from the bathroom window.

Concerned that she gets psychiatric care we don't press charges, but the police charge her for breaking and entering. After several days, I call the police to see what happened to her.

"Aw, she's OK. She's out on bail. She was on crack and alcohol. She was pretty sober by the time we got to the hospital and laughing about calling for a little boy and getting stuck in a window."

I now vigilantly lock my studio door.

Twins

by Robin Hillard

"It's a freak," Jonathon said, staring at the kitten.

"Two freaks," Samantha corrected.

"Do we have to keep it?"

"Them," Samantha corrected him again. Sitting beside me, she scratched between a pair of ginger ears then between the grey. "Of course we're keeping them."

Were my children starting one of their rare arguments?

"You could talk to the vet," Jonathon said. "If he removed one head, you'd have a normal animal."

"No!" Samantha choked on a sob. "You won't kill either cat."

Jonathon rubbed his chin with a closed fist as he watched the tiny, gently swishing tail. "It's a freak," he said again.

The kitten double purred, two heads in unanimous appreciation of Samantha's gentle hand.

"They don't think they're freaks," I said. "Nor will you, once you get used to them. Merry and Melissa." I put a finger on each little nose, names to give them personality. "You'll love them both," I assured my son.

"You do think so?"

"I know so."

There was a pause as the three of us listened to the rumble of soft purr. Samantha took after me, decisions made in a flash. She'd given her heart to the kittens at once, Jonathon needed more time.

He was like his father, slow to make up his mind, but like his father, once he accepted a responsibility, he would be utterly dependable. If only Big John were still alive to help me guide our son.

The children had plans for their afternoon, but before they left me, Jonathon reached down to scratch two tiny chins. "Merry and Melissa," he said, and I gave a silent, grateful prayer that he had accepted both the tiny heads.

"Merry and Melissa," Samantha echoed, laughing.

They left me stroking a purring bundle of fur, and I listened to the cheerful chatter as they walked out, together. My two children, on the pair of legs they shared.

Bobby Estep Made
a Big Decision

by Robb T. White

"Put it down, Estep. You ain't gonna do anything with that," John DeRosa, the store manager, said.

We were in the kitchen. I'd just come from up front where I'd been packing groceries for the last hour in one of those sheep-like rushes to the cash registers. I was trying to get a little food in me for the rest of that 12-hour day. I remember I was chewing food when he came in, the big slob, and grabbed my ass the way he did every stockboy in the store. You could be stacking cans in the aisle when he shambled past—all two-hundred-sixty pounds of him in a smock stretched tight across his gut—groping your butt.

But it was the wrong time to do that to me. I had picked up a carving knife lying on the counter. That's when he told me to put it down. I said nothing, not a word. I just stood there. Frozen. I didn't move a muscle. Instead of the arrogant tone he used with all his employees, there was the faintest quaver in his voice. That's when I realized it: *He's afraid I'm going to stick him.*

The knife swung in a perfect arc toward his neck; the blade up to the hilt just under his jawline. He didn't have time to flinch, which—thinking about it later—did surprise me.

A second passed without either of us moving. (Time stretching out in front like taffy.) His hand shot up to his neck. A ribbon of blood spurted into the air; a sheet of blood poured out between his fingers. A bellow came next: inhuman and terrifying. They told me later it was heard all the way up front by the cash registers. Customers froze in place.

My stomach churned and my knees shook at the suddenness of that one swing of my arm. Another scream erupted. Tiny red comets, colliding and passing, dotted the kitchen wall. A big bright rosette hung above the calendar.

I panicked. I thought of running, just getting the holy hell out of there, going anywhere.

I was alone in the kitchen for a long time.

No one came to look for me, none of the people who knew me as a quiet high-school kid always willing to work the long Fridays.

When the tip of the cop's shoe opened the door, I wanted to laugh.

Then I saw the barrel of his handgun aimed at my chest.

Then those words you hear on TV all the time: "Put your hands up!"

Headlights of Her Desire

by Michael Webb

As I walk in, Angela's face is hidden by a cloud of steam. She stands there, feet bare, still wearing the dress she had worn that morning, looking down into a boiling pot. The kitchen is a whirl of mess, and my Angela in the center, twirling, checking this, stirring that, barely noticing me as I shed my shoes next to hers by the door.

"So I was thinking," Angela says. She often does this, beginning a conversation as if the previous one had never stopped.

"I'm fine, thanks," I interrupt, trying to bring her up short. "And how are you?" I walk across the dining room, undressing as I walk.

"So I was thinking," Angela says louder. I change in the bedroom into a pair of loose shorts and a t-shirt from a charity run. "This is the week when I'm in the hot zone, right? According to the math?" I feel the conversation sliding into a place I don't want to go, but I am as helpless as a driver speeding around an icy curve.

"Right," I say. Angela was one for projects, and after a rash of pregnancies at the bank, fertility had become her new obsession. On Sunday, we had mapped it out and determined that this week would be her maximally fertile time. I kept my feelings locked away, nodding at her, not discouraging her.

"So it's time," she says. "This week. Now."

I swallow as I walk back into the dining room. We've been over the financial picture, and unless we can go farther into debt that I can imagine, even the most cut rate doctor is way out of our price range. The oven buzzes, and she whirls, donning an oven mitt and removing toasted garlic bread from our oven.

"I don't want to wait, Rachel." She sets the bread down.

"I know you don't, honey," I say quickly. "But we've been over this, and…"

"I asked Sam. At work."

I freeze, staring at her. She is pouring sauce onto two piles of pasta. I take the salad bowls from the counter and silently set them at the three place settings. Her idea suddenly swings into view. I am caught in the headlights of her desire.

"He's a freak," I say.

"He's not," Angela says. "He's odd, but he's sweet, and perfectly healthy, and single. And he's willing."

I try not to snort. "Of course he is," I say with too much bitterness.

"I want this," she says softly. She is looking down. "Now. Tonight. Please."

I want to argue, to dissent, to tell her of all the drawbacks, but she looks hopeful, a joy in her eyes I can't take away, and I feel a knot of nausea at the base of my throat.

The intercom buzzes.

"There he is now," she says. I try to speak, and I can't. I slide my feet back into my shoes, and I pick up my work bag, and I am out the door and down the hall.

Rotifer

by Matthew Harrison

Mr Wilson's announcement was a great disappointment.

"We'd been hoping for the white mouse," Mrs Bennet sniffed. "Susie's got one at home – show Mr. Wilson Tibbles, Susie."

"Oh, *Mum!*" Susie groaned. This was not the way to apply for a biology course.

But Mr Wilson gave a fatherly smile, and asked to see Tibbles anyway. Susie opened her phone and flicked through the photos of her pet – and Mr Wilson watched patiently. "It's always good to see our students taking nature into their hearts," he said in a kindly tone.

"So, the course...?" Mrs Bennet ventured.

"Ah." Mr Wilson spread his hands, looking if possible even more fatherly. "I'm afraid we have no more places for studying the higher animals."

He raised a warning hand. "It's not just students in our school, or in our county, but the entire nation, the world. Each student has his or her own fauna focus. I'm afraid it is a very competitive market, so to speak, and we do have to be a little bit realistic..." He now looked more like the headmaster that he was.

"So I've got to study the *rotifer?*" Susie still couldn't believe it.

"Not of course all rotifers, we couldn't give you the whole field, but the bdelloid in particular." Mr Wilson chuckled. "Quite a pedigree the little fellow has — discovered in 1696, and hasn't looked back!"

"And they live... in ponds?" Mrs Bennet quavered.

"They live everywhere! Probably some in my drink right now." Mr Wilson indicated the glass on his desk.

"*Eeugh!*" Susie exclaimed.

"Right, well if there's nothing more," Mr Wilson became businesslike, "I'll put you down for the bdelloid. There are 450 species, and you can choose one all for yourself. The bdelloid have lots of interesting features, some of them have no feet, and the female reproduces by herself."

"Susie is into feminist issues," said Mrs Bennet, trying to make the best of it.

"Excellent, excellent — lots of scope there!" Mr Wilson said. Susie glumly signed the form.

Mr Wilson put the form quickly into his out tray, rising to usher them out of the room. "I know that this might not quite match your expectations, but as I was saying earlier, we have to be realistic, and I hear that some schools," he lowered his voice, "are putting their students onto *bacteria...*"

"Oh my goodness!" exclaimed Mrs Bennet.

"Goodness indeed!" And to Susie: "At least you'll be able to see your subject with a magnifying glass!"

Mother and daughter were silent as they left. When they reached the street, Mrs Bennet said, "Your father will be disappointed, but I'm sure Mr Wilson was doing his best for us."

"It's so bloody competitive!" Susie choked down a sob.

"Now dear, not that word —" Mrs Bennet began. Seeing her daughter's distress, she gave her arm a squeeze. "It did sound interesting, you know. 'No feet' — I wonder how the little things move about. Tibbles has got feet, hasn't he...?"

"*Yes*, Mum," Susie sighed.

Throwing Herself Away

by Edward O'Dwyer

She began throwing herself away piece by piece.
She tossed her bum away first,
into one of the recycling bins outside work.
No more watching it reflected in shop windows,
following her around,
welcome as a musty smell.
She ordered a new one online,
all the way from a laboratory in Paris,
genetically engineered,
sag-proof, ripple-proof, gravity-proof,
a lifetime warranty.
But then she flung her tummy
into a neighbour's skip.
It didn't match,
dripped over the edge
of all her new, tight-fitting jeans.
She bought a new one at auction,
hard and smooth as Sivec marble,
CGI-like.

She rolled down the window one day
and threw her tits out
into the ditch.
She tore her thighs up like bills.
She left her nose on train tracks,
suitable punishment for being too big,
set her chin on fire
after tearing it off in a temper.
You should really see her now.
She looks amazing,
like photo-shopped real life,
glossy, high DPI.
She's comfortable in her skin at last.
That's all she ever wanted.

Vigil

by Alex Reece Abbott

Cirrus Kite waits in his apartment, alone, pristine binoculars in hand. Standing upstairs by the open bay window, his left leg jigs. Today he's not interested in exceptional city vistas, let alone his unexceptional neighbours. He checks his chronographic watch again. The commemorative fly-past is five minutes and twenty-four seconds late. He polishes his Leica binoculars gently with a Leica microfibre lens cleaning cloth.

The four Merlin engines close in. Bone-shaking. Soul-piercing. The unmistakable, hypnotic rumble drives out any other sound. She's huge, a lone nocturnal bird of prey, exposed in the gunmetal winter day. She floats above him: strange, dark, graceful. Makes him want to stand and stare. Makes him want to run and hide.

She flies so low that he can spot the rear gunner on his vigil. Suspended in the belly of the metal raptor, he's a fledgling crammed into a transparent egg at the tail of the fuselage.

He waves to Cirrus. Star-struck, Cirrus waves back, craning until his neck cricks.

Cirrus never got the chance to go to war, but his old man, Harry, was one of those lonely look-outs: a Tail-end Charlie, an underage farm boy who snuck into the air force. Harry never talked about it, but he named his only child after his favourite cloud formation. *One of the lucky ones –*

nothing more to say, he'd growl. Harry's selective deafness made even the easiest conversation difficult.

Cirrus knows about the men returning from the war: damaged goods, never quite fitting in, shut down by what they'd seen and what they'd done. At Harry's funeral, an old squadron pal had filled Cirrus in on The Spam Raids, when they cruised over Holland at six-hundred feet, dropping food, the starving civilians waving from every window. The Bad Penny Boys always turned up.

Until their luck ran out.

Shot down near the end of the war, Perspex running like water, a blazing wing falling off within forty-five seconds. The rush to bail out. Gunners had the lowest chances of survival. Cutting the silk parachute, he'd made a dressing for Harry's scorched face.

The bomber thunders into the distance. Cirrus wipes his eyes. He's only ever watched a Lancaster in old newsreels and he'll probably never see another one, not flying. But, he sees now. Sees Harry, going up, night after night, alone at the back of the plane. Encased in the blazing, molten cage. Sees his refusal to have a fire in the house. Sees his old man raging, making his boy run and hide.

His leg jigs. Harry might be proud of him, now he's in charge of monitoring the CCTV for the whole city. And, there's his own son, training to fly drones at a secret air-base bunker, thousands of miles from his targets. Cirrus wonders if there's a surveillance gene, some inherent, freakish, detail-loving need to watch.

He polishes his binoculars and scans the sky, hoping for one last glimpse. And, he wonders who kept vigil over Harry, the solitary look-out.

I Have an Incredible Thing

by Brad Garber

I have known this since childhood. I would like to say it is bigger and better than most, but that would not be true. I noticed it, rather gradually, over time. How it appeared, how it felt, how it became such an enormous part of my life. Sort of freaky, when you get right down to it. I always wondered if others noticed how it changed me, how it affected my sense of humor, my attitude about certain vegetables, my concerns and neuroses. What does one do with such a thing? I don't know, but it's there and I have had to learn how to deal with it. It has been, sort of, out of my hands. But, I have to admit that it really is not a burden to have to negotiate the demands posed by such a thing because, when it comes right down to it, I am simply blessed. Sometimes, my thing just takes me by surprise. Just sort of does what it wants and I have no control. It can be quite entertaining, under those circumstances. It is full of artistic talents. Sometimes, it just embarrasses me. Like that one time in the produce section of the market. To some extent, however, my thing just completes me and makes me who I am, as a human being. It is the sort of thing that, at first glance, you would not think to be just as incredibly important as it is. I can't bear to think of living without it. I would like to tell you that my thing is a good cook, or that it cleans my house, or feeds the cat. Sorry... not that physically inclined. I would like to tell you that my thing is very intellectual and a good conversationalist at a party. There are, unfortunately, just some things that my thing cannot do, on its own. I need to offer assistance, from time to time. But, that does not diminish the value of my thing. I am indebted to my thing…it has taught me so much about myself and others. Sometimes, my thing senses things that I never would have thought or cared about. Its empathetic nature, coupled with a bold and adventurous spirit, has led me down many paths that I, otherwise, would have never explored. What my thing has proven to me is that it is noble to be free and proud with what you have and what you are. But, don't let your thing control your life.

I Am So Sorry For Your Loss

by Gwendolyn Joyce Mintz

The sympathy card that Phoebe sent John F. Kennedy, Jr when his mother died was sepia-tinted with a bouquet of white irises on the front. The inside was blank. She pondered for days what to write. Every time she thought she knew what to say, she practiced it first on a sheet of notebook paper. The words had to be right because she didn't have the money for another card.

Limited finances would no longer be a problem, however, if her plan worked.

Her compassion and thoughtfulness would touch him. Lead to a whirlwind romance. End with a chocolate wedding cake. She loved chocolate cake.

When the card was returned, Phoebe was dismayed.

At the post office, the worker explained that there needed to be a numbered address and zip code. "If he lived in a small town, we maybe could find him. But you're sending it to New York City."

"But it's John F. Kennedy, Jr.! The only one in Manhattan." Her finger jabbed at the envelope on the counter between them. "Couldn't somebody just deliver it to his airport?"

The clerk sighed. "Don't freak out," he told her. "Just get us a street address."

If I knew where he lived, I'd have taken it myself, Phoebe thought as she snatched the card up.

At home, she put it aside until she could figure out what to do. She remembered it only when that photograph appeared on the news: Him kissing his new bride's hand.

Disbelief gripped her heart. She tried to console it with the words he'd never read—*I am so sorry for your loss. I am so sorry for your loss. I am so sorry for your loss*—but her heart would not be soothed. She recalled the something else she'd written.

Right now you'd probably rather die yourself than face the pain of losing the person you love.

She knew she did.

Close Encounter of the Emergency Kind

by Matt Potter

She must have been 70, thinning beige bob touching bony jade silk shoulders, and thinner skin taut across glassy cheekbones. And there she stood, slinging a box of *Siren's Song Heavy Duty* tampons down my checkout conveyor belt ... like she was born to it!

The tampons slid to a stop in front of the sensor. "It's an emergency," she whispered, and reaching across the rubber with her wrinkled fingers, she glanced at my name badge, touched me lightly on the hand, and added, "I really need the *Extra Thirsty* Heavy Duty ones, but you don't seem to stock them here, *Desirée*."

Smiling, she showed me a perfect row – an entire mouthful! – of white china caps.

"You have no idea how often this happens, *Desirée*," she sighed. "That's the problem, I'm the kind-o-gal who goes that extra mile."

I blinked. They hadn't taught me about handling this sort of customer in the retail re-training course they shoved me into after I had my meltdown collecting stats at the fail-safe nuclear shelter service.

What to do?

Pushing my purple polyester sleeve up my arm, I scratched the psoriasis scab on my elbow and thought: *Just blink again, Desirée.* So I blinked, again.

A slow toss of her head and the woman flicked her beige bob off her shoulders. And looked at me, glossy-eyed. "You must get that a lot, older women coming in for emergency tampons."

"No," I said. "Not really."

"Never?" she asked. Purring, she swung her bag off her shoulder and positioned it on the conveyor belt.

She's probably an old checkout chick, I thought, made good and wanting to lord it over me. Probably now passing herself off as an ex-TV hostess. Probably thinks I've always been a checkout chick too, wouldn't even think I used to be the senior stats collector at the fail-safe nuclear shelter service before I had that meltdown.

Yeah, I know the type ...

"I've just come from the ceremony where it was announced my recent novelette has been nominated to be nominated to be nominated for the longlist for the Pulitzer Prize." And reaching into her bag, she pulled out a ten-dollar note and pushed it across the rubber. "I'm so incredibly grateful."

She looked at me and tilted her head – well, she stared really, the fine down on her chin visible in the store's fluorescent light – chewing her cud as she waited for an answer.

I pushed the other purple polyester sleeve up my other arm, and scratched the psoriasis scab on my other elbow. Then picking up the ten dollars, I said, "Yeah, I guess there's no controlling fertility."

She pocketed the tampon pack in her bag and pulled out a business card, placing it in the palm of my hand. *Vivien-Marie Angst*, it said. *Author.* Next to a picture of her with the same hairdo and the same smile, from thirty or forty or maybe fifty years ago.

"Keep that in a safe place, Desirée," she whispered. "It'll be worth a lot of money one day."

Authors

Alex Reece Abbott

writes across genres, forms and hemispheres, and has won the Northern Crime Competition and Arvon Prize. Her short fiction often shortlists, including for the Bridport, Elbow Room, and Sunday Business Post/Penguin Short Story prizes. A finalist in the 2016 Over the Edge New Writer of the Year, her literary historical novel, *The Helpmeet* is a 2016 Greenbean Irish Novel Fair winner. Her contemporary novel, *Last of the Lucky Country*, shortlisted for the 2015 Northern Crime Competition.

Duff Allen

is a writer who lives in upstate New York. He has an MFA from Bard College where he teaches writing in The Clemente Course for the Humanities. His work appears in *Prima Materia*, *Burningword Literary Journal*, *Eunoia Review*, and many other publications,

Samantha Armatys

lives on the Gold Coast, Australia, and craves proximity to the coastline. She has recently returned from living on a small island in the Philippines. Samantha previously worked in journalism and is now completing her Honours in Creative Writing at Griffith University. She is a writer of fiction short and long, fascinated by the feminine voice in literature. *White Ink* is the first formal publication of her creative work.

David S. Atkinson

is the author of *Apocalypse All the Time* (forthcoming 2017), *Not Quite so Stories, The Garden of Good and Evil Pancakes* (2015 National Indie Excellence Awards finalist in humor), and *Bones Buried in the Dirt* (2014 Next Generation Indie Book Awards finalist, First Novel <80K). His writing appears in *Bartleby Snopes, Grey Sparrow Journal, Atticus Review*, and others. His writing website is http://davidsatkinsonwriting.com/.

Jane Banning

lives in northern Wisconsin and has had over thirty of her stories, poems, and flash fiction writings published in various journals, including the *Boston Literary Magazine*, the University of Iowa *Daily Palette*, and *Long Story Short*, among others. She was a finalist in the Glass Woman Prize and the Micro Award. Her novel, *Silo*, is looking for an agent and while it's out looking, Jane goes kayaking.

Tina Barry

has had poems and short stories appear in numerous publications, including *The Best Small Fictions 2016* (Queens Ferry Press), *Drunken Boat, Lost in Thought, Blue Fifth Notebook*, and *Exposure, an Anthology of Micro-fiction*. Two pieces in *Mall Flower* (Big Table Publishing, 2015), her first book of poems and short fiction, were nominated for Pushcart Prizes. She is a 2016 Best of the Net nominee. Find her at TinaBarryWriter.com.

Paul Beckman

was one of the winners in the 2016 Best Small Fictions with his story *Healing Time* and his 100 word story *Mom's Goodbye* was chosen as the winner of the 2016 Fiction Southeast Editor's Prize. His stories are widely published in print and online. Paul lives in Connecticut and earned his MFA from Bennington College. His published story website can be found at www.paulbeckmanstories.com and his blog at www.pincusb.com.

Irene Buckler

as a teacher, worked with young learners for over three decades. During her professional life, she concentrated on writing educational programs, stories for children and poetry. Her stories and poems have appeared in publications for children in Ireland and Australia. Irene enjoys the challenge of writing flash fiction where less is so much more.

Megan Crosbie

is a queer writer and occasional performer who lives in Scotland. She spends most of her free time writing very short fractured fairy-tales and other works of flash fiction. Her writing has been published around the world, both online and in print. When not writing she enjoys travelling, drag shows, and too much wine.

Peter DiChellis

concocts sinister and sometimes comedic tales for anthologies, ezines, and magazines. Peter is a member of the Short Mystery Fiction Society and an Active (published author) member of the Mystery Writers of America, Private Eye Writers of America, and International Thriller Writers. For

more of his work, visit his site *Murder and Fries* at
http://murderandfries.wordpress.com/.

Glen Donaldson

likes to think he wouldn't be the first to be offed in a slasher
movie. He is the creator and author of Ergon Energy's
Powersavvy Man character and stories. His work also
appears in *Donut Factory*, *Ink in Thirds*, *Fewer than 500*,
Bindweed Magazine and *Centrum Press*.

Kristina England

resides in Worcester, Massachusetts. Her writing has been
published in several magazines, including *Gargoyle*, *Muddy
River Poetry Review*, *New Verse News*, and *Silver Birch
Press*. Her first set of published photos appeared at *Foliate
Oak Literary Magazine* in April 2016.

Brad Garber

has degrees in biology, chemistry and law. He writes, paints,
draws, photographs, hunts for mushrooms and snakes, and
runs around naked in the Great Northwest. Since 1991, he
has published poetry, essays and weird stuff in such
publications as *Edge Literary Journal*, *Clementine Poetry
Journal*, *Sugar Mule*, *Barrow Street*, *Aji Magazine* and other
quality publications. He is a 2013 Pushcart Prize nominee.

Flora Gaugg

is a writer based in Adelaide, Australia. She has received
recognition for both fiction and playwriting. She is
interested in stories about ordinary people, and claims to be
remarkably ordinary herself.

Mark Govier

attended the University of Adelaide, and worked in odd jobs like bails clerk at Long Bay Prison, as a crematorium assistant, and in boring legal and government positions in London. His former father-in-law was a Sydney gangster! He's had one speculative fiction novel published, *Trials of Nian Gao*. He's also a passable social historian of science and an OK poet of really dark matters.

John Grey

is an Australian-born, US resident short storywriter and poet. He has been published in numerous magazines including *Weird Tales, Christian Science Monitor, Greensboro Poetry Review, Agni, Poet Lore* and *Journal Of The American Medical Association* as well as the horror anthology *What Fears Become* and the science fiction anthology *Futuredaze*. He was the winner of the Rhysling Award for short genre poetry in 1999.

Diana Grove

has a graduate certificate in writing from the University of New England, and lives in Perth, Australia. She has a penchant for stories that are dark and bizarre. *Robot Lover* is her first published work.

Matthew Harrison

lives in Hong Kong, and whether because of that or some other reason entirely his writing has veered from non-fiction to literary and he is currently reliving a boyhood passion for science fiction. He has published more than sixty SF short stories and is building up to longer pieces as he learns more about the universe. Matthew is married with two children but no pets. Find more at www.matthewharrison.hk.

Robin Hillard

lives in Toowoomba, also known as the "Garden City" of Queensland. It is well served with antique shops, and these provided the inspiration for the problems that bedevil the customers and staff of Archie's Antiques, short mysteries which originally appeared in the ezine *Bonzer!* and were later picked up by Cyberworld Publishing. Toowoomba also provided a setting for her mystery novel *Ridgeway Murder.*

Stephen House

has had many plays commissioned/produced, won two Awgie Awards, an Adelaide Fringe Award and been shortlisted for the Patrick White Playwright & Queensland Premier Drama awards, and the Tom Collins and Rhonda Jankovic Poetry Awards. He recently won second in The Sawmiller's Poetry Prize. He has received Australia Council Canada and Ireland literature residencies, and an Asialink grant. He has seen his plays and poems published and performed nationally/internationally.

Mark Hudson

is a writer, artist, and was once referred to as a freak. (Who wasn't?) But as he said to a fellow artist yesterday, "Us artists and writers are the normal people these days!" Mark likes science fiction, eccentric short stories and quirky things. And even though he was called "weird" as a youth, he never thought there would come a day when the world would be weirder than his imagination was. He lives in the U.S.A, where he is "freaking out" over the presidential election result...

A.J. Huffman

has had poetry, fiction, haiku, and photography appear in hundreds of national and international journals, including *Labletter, The James Dickey Review,* and *Offerta Speciale,* in which her work appeared in both English and Italian translation. She is also the founding editor of Kind of a Hurricane Press: www.kindofahurricanepress.com.

Hasen Hull

lives in London. His work has appeared in *Litro, Dirty Chai, Flash Fiction Press, Praxis* and elsewhere. He enjoys photography and long journeys.

Phillis Ideal

both writes and paints, finding one no easier than the other. Her short stories are based on NYC and New Mexico experiences. She exhibits her paintings in the USA and Europe and splits her time between NYC and Santa Fe. Her stories have also been published on *Fictionaut, Santa Fe Literary Review* and *Eunola Review.* Your can find her at http://www.phillisideal.com.

Em Koenig

is a queer poet/DJ/Winter Witch from Adelaide. Their work has featured in *On Dit, Flazeda, Uneven Floor,* et. al. They have participated in spoken word events as part of Feast Festival and in 2016 contributed work to the 'Queering The Museum' event at the South Australian Migration Museum. Em is currently working on the collaborative music/performance/writing project Climate of Cruelty, which explores the links between the factory farming industry and the destruction of the environment. Find more at www.climateofcruelty.com.

Donna Krause

lives in the suburbs in Willow Grove, Pennsylvania. She has a BA in sociology from Gwynned Mercy College, and has experience as a mental health therapist. She has suffered bipolar disorder for many years, and writes straight from the heart, often about her experience with her mental illness. An active participant in a weekly writing rouop, Donna has also been published in Twisted Sister and Transcendent Visions.

Len Kuntz

is a writer from Washington State, an editor at the online magazine *Literary Orphans*, and the author of *I'm Not Supposed to be Here and Neither are You* out now from *Unknown Press*. You can also find more of his work here: lenkuntz.blogspot.com.

John Lambremont, Sr.

is a poet and writer from Baton Rouge, Louisiana, U.S.A. His poems have been published internationally in many reviews and anthologies, including *Pacific Review*, *The Minetta Review*, *Flint Hills Review*, and *Clarion*, and he has been nominated for The Pushcart Prize. John's new full-length poetry volume, *The Moment Of Capture*, will be published in June 2017 by Lit Fest Press.

Kathryn Lee

is a writer of serious stuff in her day job and tries to make amends by writing creative non-fiction, short fiction and flash fiction on the weekends. Based in Western Australia, she has had pieces published in the *Jukebox* anthology produced by the Out of the Asylum writers' group and the literary magazine, *Cuttlefish*.

Lucy M. Logsdon

has had work appear in such publications as *Nimrod, Literary Orphans, Heron Tree, Poet Lore, Southern Poetry Review, Iodine, Sixfold, Seventeen, Conclave, Drafthorse, Right Hand Pointing, Rust & Moth* and *Gingerbread Literary Review*. Recipient of a Macdowell Writers' Colony fellowship, she received her MFA from Columbia University. Now back in rural America, she raises chickens, ducks and other occasional creatures with her husband, and two rebel step-grrrls.

JP Lundstrom

grew up and attended college in southern California. Her writing most often is set in that warm, often dangerous place known as Los Angeles during the mid-twentieth century. Current books are *Adventures of a Young Girl* and *The Fruit of the Poisonous Tree*, both available on Kindle. She strives for easy reading, not that intellectual stuff; she doesn't like to waste time on deep thoughts.

Catfish McDaris

has been active in the small press world for 25 years. His biggest seller is *Prying*, with Jack Micheline and Charles Bukowski. He's working in a wig shop in a high crime area of Milwaukee. His newest book *Sleeping with the Fish* can be bought through Amazon.com.

Gwendolyn Joyce Mintz

is an award-winning writer and a photographer. Her work has appeared in various journals and she is the author of two chapbooks, *Mother Love* and *Where I'll Be If I'm Not There*. She (infrequently) blogs about her creative endeavors at http://wwwonewriter.blogspot.com.

Richie Narvaez

has had work published in *Faultline*, *Mississippi Review*, *Out of the Gutter 8*, *Pilgrimage*, and *Sunshine Noir*. His book of short fiction, *Roachkiller and Other Stories*, won the 2013 Spinetingler Award for Best Anthology/Short Story Collection. Find more at http://www.richienarvaez.com.

Pádraig Ó Cúana

is a Brisbane-based composer, whose works have been performed from Melbourne to San Francisco. When he is not composing classical repertoire, Pádraig is passionate about reading and writing poetry. His early influences were the likes of Ginsberg and Bukowski, whilst the Ulster Cycle has been a recent source of inspiration in his music and poetry alike. Pádraig is currently studying the use of spoken word in chamber music.

Edward O'Dwyer

from Limerick, Ireland, has poetry published in magazines and anthologies throughout the world, such as *The Forward Book of Poetry*, *Poetry Ireland Review*, *The Manchester Review*, *A Hudson View Poetry Digest*, *The Houston Literary Review*, and many others. His debut collection, *The Rain on Cruise's Street* (2014), is published by Salmon Poetry, from which the follow-up is due early 2017. He is an editor for Revival Press, a community publishing house in Limerick. He was selected in 2010 by Poetry Ireland for their Introduction Series. He has been shortlisted for a Hennessy Award, the Desmond O'Grady Prize and the North West Words Prize, among others. His work has been nominated for Forward, Pushcart, and Best of the Web prizes and is translated into Slovene and Romanian.

Carl 'Papa' Palmer

of Old Mill Road in Ridgeway VA now lives in University Place WA. He has a 2015 Seattle Metro contest-winning poem riding buses somewhere in Emerald City. Carl, president of The Tacoma Writers Club, is a Pushcart Prize and Micro Award nominee. His motto is Long Weekends Forever. Find more at www.authorsden.com/carlpalmer.

Joseph S. Pete

once googled the Iowa Writers Workshop. He is an award-winning journalist and Iraq War veteran who won second place for poetry in the PBR Art Contest and first place at BaconFest Chicago 2016, feats that Milton chump never accomplished. The Indiana University graduate's work has appeared in *Dogzplot*, *Zero Dark Thirty*, *Punchnel's*, *McSweeney's Internet Tendency*, *365 Tomorrows*, *Pulp Modern*, *The Higgs Weldon*, *Gutzine* and elsewhere.

Ben Pitts

is from Phoenix, Arizona. He is a High School English teacher by day and a renegade poet by night. He lives with his wife, Brianne and daughter, Grace. His poetry has been featured on several websites and journals including *Pure Slush's* journals, *Tall...ish*, *Summer*, and most recently in *The Machinery* literary collection. He looks forward to pursuing his MFA in creative writing and finishing his poetry collection.

Martin Jon Porter

is a 34-year-old teacher who lives in Brunswick, Melbourne. His poetry has featured in Australian literary journals and magazines as well as the USA. His debut chapbook, *Traits*, has recently been published by Ginninderra Press as part of its Picaro Poets series. In a world saturated with the moving image, he still believes in ones derived from stationary stimulus.

Matt Potter

is an Australian-born writer who keeps a part of his psyche in Berlin. Matt has been published in various places online, and you can find more of his work including details of his travel memoir *Hamburgers and Berliners and other courses in between* (Cervena Barva Press, 2015), his collections *Vestal Aversion* (Pure Slush Books, 2012) and *Based on True Stories* (Truth Serum Press, 2016), and his ESL teaching resources *all you need is ... a whiteboard, a marker and this book Volumes 1 and 2* (Everytime Press, 2016), at his website http://mattcpotter.webs.com/.

Melisa Quigley

is a writer and poet who finished a degree in Professional Writing and Editing at RMIT University in 2015. Her poetry has appeared in *Memory Weaving* and *Tall...ish* and she also has a short story published in *Frayed*. You can find further examples of her work at her website here: melisaquigley.wordpress.com.

Stephen V. Ramey

lives in beautiful New Castle, Pennsylvania, with his wife and two reformed feral cats. His work has appeared in many places, including *The Journal of Compressed Creative Arts*, *The Doctor T. J. Eckleburg Review*, and *Every Day Fiction*. His collection of (very) short fictions, *Glass Animals* (Pure Slush Books), is available wherever fine books are e-sold. More at www.stephenvramey.com and on facebook and twitter (@svramey).

Alex Robertson

spent his formative years in Adelaide and worked his early waged life around (country) South Australia and the Northern Territory. He has been published in university student publications and more recently in print and online journals. Since his location to the Adelaide Plains he has been involved in writing groups and broadcasting organisations around the North East suburbs of Adelaide and Gawler.

Jennifer Rose

lives with her husband in a small town inland from the first white-man-settled place on the south coast of Western Australia. She teaches English part time in the local secondary school. Her Christian faith underpins her life.

Ruth Sabath Rosenthal

is a New York City poet, well published in the U.S. and, also, internationally. In October 2006, her poem 'on yet another birthday' was nominated for a Pushcart prize. She has authored five books: *Facing Home; Facing Home and beyond; little, but by no means small; Food: Nature vs Nurture;* and *Gone, but Not Easily Forgotten.* The books are available from Amazon.com. Find Ruth's website at http://www.newyorkcitypoet.com and her blogsite at http://www.poetrybyruthsabathrosenthal.com.

Andrew Stancek

entertains Muses in southwestern Ontario. His work has appeared in *Tin House* online, *Journal of Compressed Creative Arts, Vestal Press, Necessary Fiction, Every Day Fiction,* fwriction and *Camroc Press Review,* among others. He's been a winner in the *Flash Fiction Chronicles* and

Gemini Fiction Magazine contests and been nominated for a Pushcart Prize.

J. J. Steinfeld

lives on Prince Edward Island, where he is patiently waiting for Godot's arrival and a phone call from Kafka. While waiting, he has published seventeen books, including *Disturbing Identities* (Stories, Ekstasis Editions), *Would You Hide Me?* (Stories, Gaspereau Press), *Misshapenness* (Poetry, Ekstasis Editions), *Identity Dreams and Memory Sounds* (Poetry, Ekstasis Editions), *Madhouses in Heaven, Castles in Hell* (Stories, Ekstasis Editions), and *An Unauthorized Biography of Being* (110 Short Fictions Hovering Between the Absurd and the Existential, Ekstasis Editions).

Dianne Turner

lives in Hervey Bay, Queensland and between studying and working she writes poetry, stories, articles and essays that she hopes to get published in the future. She recently completed a Bachelor of Arts in Professional Writing and Publishing with Curtin University. Dianne has had poems published in 2015 *Grieve Anthology* for Hunters Writer's Centre, *The d'Verse Anthology* for Dverse Poets Community and other poetry and stories published under her previous name Buckman.

Rob Walker

rob walker *(n)*

pron./rob wȯkə/

1. a cantankerous curmudgeon with a titanium knee
2. an original cliché
3. www.robwalkerpoet.com

Michael Webb

is proud to be published in a number of *Pure Slush* titles while he sells drugs outside Philadelphia, Pennsylvania.

Anne E. Weisgerber

has been published in *Structo Magazine*, *SmokeLong Quarterly*, *The Collapsar*, *Entropy Magazine*, *DIAGRAM*, *Shotgun Honey*, and *Jellyfish Review*. *The Airgonaut* has nominated her for *Best of the Net*, and she is a *Best Small Fictions* 2016 Finalist. She reads for *Pithead Chapel*, and reviews for *Change Seven* and *The Review Review*. Follow her @aeweisgerber, or visit http://anneweisgerber.com.

Andrew West

is Bangkok-based and author of *Thai Neotraditional Art* (2015), *Destiny to Imagination* (2013), an art fiction novel published in the Thai language in 2008 and the forthcoming *Time Beings*, a novel to be released by Double Dragon in 2017. He has penned numerous short stories and articles. His solo art exhibition, Three Worlds, was shown at the prestigious BACC in 2014. West studied writing at Western Sydney University, graduating with an MA.

Robb T. White

has published a dozen short stories and three hardboiled private-eye novels featuring series character Thomas Haftmann. His ebook crime novel, *Special Collections*, won the New Rivers Electronic Book Competition in 2014. His latest Haftmann novel is *Nocturne for Madness* (New Pulp, 2016) and a recent collection of crime stories is *Dangerous Women: Stories of Crime, Mystery, and Mayhem*. Find his website at tomhaftmann.wixsite.com/robbtwhite.

Allan J. Wills

"He moves through life with an odd kick to his gallop."
"He's old, fat and lazy."
He tries to create a path to the emotional truth in his writing.
Sometimes that involves deviating from reality.
He prefers the medium of flash fiction.

Other books from Pure Slush

Visit the Pure Slush Store:
http://pureslush.webs.com/store.htm

Feast!
ISBN: 978-1-925101-62-1

Five
ISBN: 978-1-925101-71-3

tall...ish
ISBN: 978-1-925101-80-5

Summer
ISBN: 978-1-925536-13-3

Rattle of Want
ISBN: 978-1-925101-67-6

Many Fish to Fry
ISBN: 978-1-925101-59-1

www.ingramcontent.com/pod-product-compliance
Lightning Source LLC
Chambersburg PA
CBHW052148170626
46812CB00004B/1633